OUT *of the* BLUE

Val Rutt lives in London where she divides her time between writing and teaching.

To find out more, visit her website:
www.valrutt.com

VAL RUTT

OUT *of the* BLUE

PICCADILLY PRESS • LONDON

First published in Great Britain in 2009
by Piccadilly Press Ltd,
5 Castle Road, London NW1 8PR
www.piccadillypress.co.uk

Text copyright © Val Rutt, 2009

A catalogue record for this book is available
from the British Library

ISBN: 978 1 84812 014 3

1 3 5 7 9 10 9 8 6 4 2

Printed in the UK by CPI Bookmarque, Croydon, CR0 4TD
Typeset by Carolyn Griffiths, Cambridge
Cover design by Simon Davis
Cover photo © Corbis

Every effort has been made to contact the copyright
holders to gain permission for the use of
copyright material in this book.

*For my mother
and in
memory of
Jean and Laurie*

August 2006

The letter is unexpected. Its arrival, in this hot summer where nothing much has happened, is startling. There has been no hint of change; no sign of cloud in the blue morning sky for a month. And then the letter arrives.

Dear Kitty Danby,

If this letter finds you, and you are the person I am looking for, then I hope that it's okay to ask you some things about the war. I believe that you knew my grandfather Samuel Ray Bailey. I am trying to find out about the time he spent in England during World

War Two where he saw active service as a fighter pilot
in the Air Force. I found your address in the back of
his pilot's logbook and it would be great if you could
give me any information you might have. I need to
find out for a school assignment and I am real
interested in history.

Yours sincerely,
John F. Bailey Rowe

Kitty looks out through the window and sees five
starlings swagger across the parched lawn.
Something disturbs them and they take off in a
group, leaving the garden empty. Kitty continues to
stare but she does not see. She is remembering the
summer evening that she met Sammy Ray Bailey.

May 1944

The hedges were high and dense, a tangle of bramble and honeysuckle winding through the hawthorn. Kitty was cycling home from choir. It was deliciously cool pedalling slowly in the shade with the breeze lifting the hair from her forehead.

She had borrowed Charlie's bicycle because she had been late; usually she walked. Last week, dawdling home, she had discovered a nest and four tiny gaping birds. Now, repeating the journey by bicycle, she hoped to see the birds again.

She watched the hedge not the road, aware even as she did it that it was foolish, but pleased to be getting away with it. She took furtive glances ahead and adjusted her course, then continued to gaze back into the hedgerow. As the greenery flitted past, she stared hard into the tiny shadows of space, trying to catch sight of a bird or a nest. Beneath her the wheels whirred and crackled on the grit. She turned the pedals as slowly as she could while keeping upright, and the bicycle wobbled and snaked along, until, at last, the front wheel rose awkwardly over a hump in the road and Kitty lost control of the machine.

As Kitty yanked hard on the handlebar and the bicycle veered wildly into the middle of the road, her stomach felt the wash of fear. Even so, the thought arrived in her head that this was inevitable; had been bound to happen. She began struggling to regain control, but her movements were too jerky and sudden – the bicycle was completely independent of her and gathering speed on a decline.

And so she was partly resigned to her fate, even as she attempted to keep her feet on the spinning pedals and resist the force that lifted her from the seat. When she took off over the handlebars, Kitty became curiously aware of the brilliant sunshine in the blue sky above her. She registered the beauty around her and somehow had time to hear and see where a distant skylark sang and hovered. She experienced the briefest moment of weightlessness followed by a sickening rush as she fell. Then she hit the ground – although it felt to her that the road hit her. As if she had been still, suspended in space and the road had been swung at her like a gigantic cricket bat.

Kitty was lying in the road when Sammy found her a few minutes later. He heard her crying as he turned the corner. He quickened his pace and stooped to a crouch at her side.

'Shh, shh, hey you're okay, let me help you.'

She was slight and dark and her hair was a mess of half-tamed curls. Blood was running from both her knees, down her shins and as she wept she turned her arms and placed a hand to her side then her head, searching out the places that hurt her.

'Ow ow ow,' she moaned through her tears as Sammy helped her to her feet. He steadied her and told her to 'hold tight' while he picked up the bicycle. 'It's in a bit of a mess – the wheel's buckled,' he said.

Charlie's bicycle. Charlie's pride and joy.

'It's not mine,' she sobbed.

'Yeah, I figured that,' he said. 'It's not a girls' bike,' then, as if seeing her properly for the first time and realising his mistake, he corrected himself. 'I mean, it's not a ladies' bike.'

Kitty limped towards where he held the bicycle.

'It's my brother Charlie's and he'll kill me. I never asked him if I could use it.'

They stood with the bicycle between them and she was still crying though she was trying to be quiet. He told her later how her eyes had amazed him – they were large, set far apart and so dark they appeared to be black. And the tears literally pooled up and overflowed in a way that had suddenly struck him as funny. Afraid he would laugh out loud, he looked down at the bicycle.

'Well, I can fix it up for you if you like.'

'Oh, do you think you could?'

'Sure thing!' He was smiling at her and Kitty blinked away tears and looked at him for the first time. His smile made him handsome and Kitty was suddenly self-conscious and dismayed. His accent and the khaki uniform he wore told her that he was an American pilot. Heat began to prickle her scalp and she could feel her nose running. Trying to wipe her face discreetly, she glanced down at her legs. Both knees were grazed and the blood was drying on her shins. She felt a new discomfort as the breeze stung the torn skin.

'Well, I'd better get home now,' she murmured and made to take the bicycle from him. He held on to it.

'Look, I'll come with you – make sure you're okay.'

Kitty hung her head, she thought of saying no and sending him away, but she did not want to be rude. So she murmured her thanks, sniffed and nodded her head. Since her sixteenth birthday she had been feeling grown-up. She had started styling her hair and wearing a little face powder. She considered herself to have made the transition to womanhood. Here she was, alone with a handsome American serviceman – a situation if ever there was one that called for a girl to be ladylike and dignified – and she had two grazed knees and had bawled like a baby. Her hair that she had carefully brushed and pinned was hanging round her face. She needed to blow her nose, but she had tucked her handkerchief into the leg of her knickers and couldn't imagine how she might retrieve it. Which just went to show, she thought miserably, how much of a child she still was – when would a grown woman ever go rummaging in her knickers for her hankie?

Sammy lifted the bicycle and put it through a gap in the hedge where it couldn't be seen from the road.

'I'll come by and get it later,' he said. Then, 'Can you walk? Is it far?' He offered his arm and Kitty let him lead her down the hill to Aunt Vi's house. She walked with her head down and noticed her scuffed shoes and the rhythmic throb of pain in her knees.

'Do you remember what happened? Did you hit a pothole?' he asked.

'I was . . . I wasn't paying attention.' Kitty's voice came out in a feeble croak and added to the things that made her wretched. She could not believe how suddenly and utterly the day had changed from good to bad.

Choir practice had been fun. In between songs, Dora had whispered that her sister was coming home for the weekend and had promised to help her alter her clothes. Gwendolyn knew all about London fashion. Dora could barely wait for the end of each song, before grabbing Kitty's arm and chattering about skirt lengths, box pleats and necklines. Her excitement was infectious and Kitty had left the hall grinning, with an invitation to spend Saturday afternoon dressmaking with Dora and Gwendolyn.

Then the lanes had been so beautiful and the bicycle had given her a sense of freedom. Kitty had felt that the world was good and life worth living, despite the war and all the bad things that could happen. And now everything had gone wrong. Charlie was going to be so angry with her and most probably Uncle Geoff would too. And as for being discovered in such a mess by an American pilot, the humiliation was unbearable. Without meaning to, Kitty groaned aloud.

'I'm sorry, I'm making you go way too fast – does it hurt a lot?' Sammy stopped walking and Kitty glanced up to see his brow furrowed with concern. Kitty felt another wave of heat rise through her face as she mumbled an apology for making a fuss.

'Hey now, it's okay – it must hurt, I can see that. Will your mother be at home?'

'No, she doesn't live there – I mean, I live with my aunt and uncle. My aunt will be there; well, at least she should be – um, she, she usually is.' Kitty clamped her mouth tight shut and shuddered at the way the words had stumbled awkwardly from her mouth. What was she doing? Why could she not put a simple sentence together?

'I'm sorry, miss . . . I didn't mean to . . .'

Kitty had enough wits left to notice his embarrassment and managed to pull herself together.

'My name's Kitty,' she said as brightly as she could, 'Kitty Danby, and my brother and I live with our aunt and uncle but our mother is still living at our home in London. We came here during the Blitz, to be safe, you see.' She looked up and for a moment stared straight into his eyes before quickly lowering her gaze.

He held out his hand. 'Pleased to meet you, Kitty. My name is Sammy, Sammy Ray Bailey.'

Kitty put her hand in his. 'I'm pleased to meet you too,' she said, and this time her voice came out all right.

They carried on walking down the hill and, as the chimneys of the first of the houses appeared through the tops of the trees, Sammy spoke. 'It was pretty bad for folks in London from '40–'41?' Kitty nodded and he continued. 'We got to see some of the newsreels at the movies. I came over back then, end of '41. I was seventeen. My Uncle Joe flew in the last war – still flies, does crop spraying, or did. He first took me up when I was five years old; let me have a go on the controls when I was ten.'

'It must be amazing to look down on the world – like the birds,' Kitty said.

'That's it, that's exactly it: you're as free as a bird and the whole world looks small and tidy.' He had turned his face towards hers and smiled broadly as he spoke, but then he frowned and shrugged and added quietly, 'Well, that's how I used to feel, you know, back in Pennsylvania when I was a kid.'

Kitty pointed ahead. 'That's Uncle Geoff and Aunt Vi's place there.'

As they approached, the front door swung open and a middle-aged woman stepped out to meet them. She dried her hands on her apron and her pale eyes widened as she took in the state that Kitty was in. Kitty murmured her thanks to Sammy and moved quietly into the hallway and stood behind her aunt.

Aunt Vi made no attempt to be discreet as she took a moment to study the young man who had brought her niece home. She eyed him up and down while

Kitty explained that he had found her hurt in the road and had insisted on helping her. Aunt Vi nodded as she listened and at last her face softened and she smiled. She shook his hand and asked Sammy in for tea. The young American declined.

When Aunt Vi heard that he was going to fix Charlie's bicycle, she insisted that he would stay for tea on Sunday afternoon when he planned to return it. This invitation he accepted with a wide grin, a nod of the head and a 'Thank you, ma'am', in a voice so warm that Kitty felt the glow from it on her skin and some previously unknown source of happiness stirred in her.

After Sammy had left, they went through to the kitchen and Aunt Vi pulled out a chair and sat Kitty down at the table.

'Well, you hear all sorts, but he was a thoroughly charming young man, I thought. Lucky for you, Kitty, that he came along when he did.'

Aunt Vi took an enamel bowl from behind the curtain under the sink. It roared like homemade percussion as she half-filled it with a jet of water from the tap. She placed the bowl on the kitchen table then, taking a cloth to the range, she lifted the kettle from the heat and warmed the water with a splash from its steaming spout.

'Now, young lady, let me clean up those grazes while you tell me what happened.'

Aunt Vi crouched down and Kitty winced as she lifted a flannel from the warm water and began wiping away the blood and grit.

'Charlie's bicycle went out of control.'

'You shouldn't've had Charlie's bicycle, Kit – we'll never hear the end of it.'

'I know.'

Aunt Vi took the top off a tube of Valderma antiseptic and Kitty reached out and took it from her. The back door opened abruptly and Uncle Geoff came in and plopped a rabbit in the sink.

'What's happened to you, Kit – been fighting the war have you?'

Aunt Vi left Kitty to apply her own antiseptic and stood up.

'Oooh, what a whopper – we'll have a stew. Young Kitty's taken a fall from Charlie's bicycle. It's come off worse than Kitty has, by the sound of it.'

'Eh? And what does Charlie have to say about that?'

'He doesn't know yet. A nice American lad – pilot from the airbase, he found Kitty and he's going to mend the bicycle.'

Uncle Geoff had hold of the rabbit and was working his fingers under the skin tearing the fur from the flesh.

'Not a young'un this, Vi, he'll need longer in the pot.'

'I don't think I need you to tell me how to cook a rabbit,' Aunt Vi grumbled.

'I was just saying.' He took up his knife and cut the skin from the animal's legs. 'You want to watch the Yanks, Kitty. They took their time getting into this war, but in other ways they're not backwards in coming forwards, if you know what I mean.'

Before Kitty could reply, Charlie came through the front door shouting.

'Kitty, are you all right? Mrs Parkes said she saw you coming home with a Yank and you were covered in blood —'

Charlie had reached the kitchen and looked with disappointment at Kitty.

'You look fine,' he said. 'What'ya do anyway?'

Aunt Vi turned away from him and joined

Uncle Geoff at the sink. Kitty stood up carefully.

'I'm really sorry, Charlie. I've crashed your bicycle. Only it's all right – it'll get fixed.'

'My bicycle? Of course you crashed it – you're just a stupid girl. I never said you could ride it anyway. Where is it? I hate you, Kitty. If you've —!' Charlie had raised his hands as if he was considering grabbing his sister by the throat. He was a year younger than her but already he was a head and shoulders taller.

'Now, that's enough. Leave your sister alone,' snapped Uncle Geoff.

Aunt Vi stepped in now and herded Charlie towards the far end of the table where a bench stood beneath the window.

'Sit down and calm yourself. An American pilot is bringing your bicycle over on Sunday. It's not damaged at all – he brought Kitty home and couldn't manage the bicycle as well that's all. It'll be good as new when you see it – you'll not know the difference. And you'll get to meet a pilot into the bargain. I'm thinking it's you as should be thanking Kitty. Now eat this bit of bread up and let's not have any of your nonsense.' As she spoke, she cut and buttered a slice from a loaf and gave it to Charlie. The bread was still warm and normally Aunt Vi wouldn't allow it to be cut until the old loaf was finished. Kitty sat down quietly and marvelled at Aunt Vi's powers of persuasion and her economy with the truth.

Uncle Geoff had finished skinning the rabbit and he placed it on the table. Its rose pink flesh was marbled here and there with purple and a few yellow-white threads of fat.

'There you go – supper!' he announced proudly.

'Tomorrow's dinner more like – we've got leftovers to use up,' replied Aunt Vi. 'Now, do you think you could all get out from under my feet while I get Mr Bun here in a pot?'

Charlie left the kitchen and Kitty followed him.

'I'm really very sorry, Charlie – I shouldn't have taken it, I know that – I wasn't thinking – I should've asked you.'

'Derrick probably would've let you borrow it. He liked you.'

Kitty hesitated, unsure what to say. Charlie hadn't mentioned Derrick in a long time.

'Did he?' she said quietly.

'He said he was going to marry you when we grew

up. Only so as he and I could be brothers, mind you – I don't think he was ever soppy for you, nothing like that. But I know he would have let you ride the bicycle if you'd asked him.'

Kitty thought about what she wanted to say next and wondered if she dared say it. She imagined saying, *Do you miss him?* In the end she said, 'He was a nice boy.'

Charlie didn't answer but made a small muffled noise in his throat. He had his face turned away from her and Kitty raised her hand and faltered, unsure whether to touch him or not. As she hesitated, Charlie suddenly sprung forward and raced up the stairs.

'The bicycle better be all right, Kitty!' he called down to her before slamming his bedroom door.

May 1941

It had been a cloudless night in London and the moon was full when the Danby family went to the Anderson shelter in the garden. After the all-clear in the morning they emerged into a haze. Charlie only once described to Kitty what happened to him that day.

The news that there were direct hits down the street was yelled across garden hedges, and Charlie was desperate to go and see for himself and look for shrapnel for his collection. As soon as they got back into the house, Charlie ran upstairs saying that they should start breakfast without him. He banged the toilet door and slid the bolt noisily. Then he held his breath as he pushed against the door and silently released the bolt.

Charlie crept down the first few steps of the staircase and leaned over the banister rail. He could hear his mum talking and he could see Kitty's legs as she moved backwards and forwards. *Good,* he thought. They were busy in the kitchen. He raced down the stairs and had the front door open and was halfway through it before he called back, 'Just nipping out, Mum, back in a jiffy!'

Charlie slammed the door as his mum's voice chased him into the front garden.

'Charlie! Don't you . . .'

But Charlie put the door between his ears and the voice and he didn't get to hear the end of the sentence. *You're not really doing anything wrong if you've not quite heard what it is you're not supposed to do*, he thought cheerfully, and felt a thrilling little skip in his stomach.

Charlie was out of the gate at a run and hurtling round to Derrick Painter's house. He had heard his mum say earlier that number seventeen had been hit during the night raid. That was where Derrick's nana and grandad lived – they normally slept in a

Morrison shelter in the front room, but they had been having their tea at Derrick's house when the siren sounded and had spent the night in Derrick's Anderson shelter. Kitty had said how lucky they were not to be at home when the bomb struck. But their mum had said, 'It's come to something when you're lucky you've had your house flattened.'

As Charlie turned the corner, he saw Derrick running up the road towards him.

'Me grandad's meeting the ARP man at the house in fifteen minutes – they're gonna board up the downstairs windows. We've gotta be quick, Charlie. I'll cop it if Grandad sees us there.'

Puffing and red-faced, Derrick collided with Charlie and began pushing him back round the corner. Charlie wriggled free.

'I was going to say we should go round the block and come up from the bottom of Hope Street. If me mum or Kitty sees us heading that way they'll stop us.'

But Derrick shrugged him off and kept going. 'There's no time to go all the way round – come on!'

The two boys slowed down when they reached Charlie's house and crossed the road. Once they were past it, they ran as fast as they could until they were opposite number seventeen before crossing back.

Derrick's grandparents' house was an end of terrace and the bomb had hit the gable end. The front of the house was still standing, but the roof was gone and there was a gaping hole in the side. The rubble beneath the hole was smoking. Despite this chaos, the front gate was latched and most of the garden was neat and tidy. The two boys peered over the fence. Derrick was the first to speak.

'Look at that.' Derrick pointed at a pile of clothes that lay strewn across the path by the front door. 'That's my grandad's best suit, that is.'

Glancing up and down the street, Charlie unlatched the gate and went into the front garden and walked towards the smouldering pile of bricks. He picked his way down the side passage into the back garden. Here, there was a much bigger mound of bricks and rubble where the back of the house had taken the impact of the blast. Looking up, he could see the interior wall of the back bedroom. It was peculiar to see the wallpaper, pink regency stripes that no one but Derrick's grandparents had looked at since it was hung, now exposed for all to see. Charlie saw what was left of the wardrobe; the splintered wood slumped to one side and the clothes bulging out.

Charlie wasn't aware of Derrick who had walked past him and stepped over the bricks and into the back room. His nana called it the dining room, but it was really the most used room of the house, where they ate their meals, read the paper, listened to the radio and sat together when there wasn't a raid.

'Streuth!' Derrick murmured as he looked at the table crushed beneath the weight of the fallen bricks and plaster. 'They can't live here no more.'

As Charlie turned his attention to where Derrick was standing, he saw the cast-iron fireplace in the bedroom above hanging from the wall at a forty-five degree angle over Derrick's head.

'Get out! It's not safe!'

Derrick turned his face and grinned at Charlie. And then, what remained of the ceiling, the bedroom wall and the fireplace collapsed in a sickening roaring rush.

The following week, on the day of Derrick's funeral, Mr and Mrs Painter received a telegram. Their elder son, Reg, had been killed at sea. The next day Mrs Danby made the arrangements to send her children to her brother and his wife in Kent and went to the town hall and volunteered for war work.

'Pack your bags, you two – you're going to stay with Auntie Vi and Uncle Geoff in the country.'

'Aren't you coming with us, Mum?' Kitty asked.

'I'll take you down and stay the night, but I'm starting work on Monday in the munitions factory.'

Kitty had looked over at Charlie, but he had his face turned to the window and he said nothing.

The morning that Kitty and Charlie were set to catch the train to Ashford, Derrick's father had wheeled the bicycle round. It had belonged to Reg.

'Since Derrick's not here to ride it, we want you to have it.'

Mr Painter put an arm round Charlie's shoulders and led him up the path. Mrs Painter stood beside the bicycle where it leaned against the lamppost.

Charlie started crying. He hung his head, held his hands loosely by his side and cried.

'Now lad, come on,' said Mr Painter. 'I've put the seat down a bit for you. Derrick would have wanted it – you see now? Don't take on or you'll upset Mrs Painter and she's got enough sorrow. Good lad.'

Charlie had covered his eyes with his forearm and gasped for air. Then he staggered forward and took hold of the handlebars.

'That's it, lad, on you get, try it out. You'll get a hang of the gears, you'll see.'

Kitty had watched from the gate. She saw Charlie's trembling back as he wobbled away on the bicycle. One of his grey socks had slipped down to his ankle.

August 2006

Kitty lifts her knitting from her workbox. The needles dip and click and Kitty sits and remembers Charlie. He had a thing about his socks being pulled up. She recalls how, when their socks became worn and loose through washing, their mother sewed circles of elastic to wear as garters. *We made do in those days,* she thinks, *we had to. And we had no say in things back then.* Kitty marvels for a moment at the things children had to put up with. Kitty and Charlie went to stay with Uncle Geoff and Aunt Vi in May 1941. For years Kitty assumed that they had been sent away because of the Blitz getting worse. She had rightly guessed that what had happened to Derrick Painter had at last convinced their mother that London was too dangerous. It wasn't until she was a mother herself that Kitty was able to imagine the rest of it. That Winifred Danby could not bear to have Charlie grow up where Dolly and Bill Painter might see him. How every sprint with a ball, every errand he ran, every time he laughed or yelled in their presence, the Painters would feel anew the pain of their loss and Win Danby would feel another pang of unbearable guilt. Kitty stirs herself from these thoughts. It doesn't do to brood on the sadness of things long past.

Kitty resumes her knitting, but soon, looking up for a moment, her eyes are drawn across the room to the mantelpiece. She checks the time and sees the letter protruding from behind the carriage clock. She hears the clock ticking and she stays perfectly still, her needles poised and thinks again of Sammy. *Sammy Ray Bailey*. She finishes the row and puts the knitting away. *Sammy Ray Bailey*.

Kitty is smiling as she waits for the kettle to boil. She says his name slowly out loud. 'Sammy Ray

Bailey.' She can see his face as clear as day. She ponders for a moment, then smiles again because she can hear his voice too. She decides, while she drinks her tea, to phone Bert Wright's daughter. Bert will know the things a boy would like to hear about his grandfather. As she passes the letter she taps its edge gently with her finger.

Kitty sits on the studded leather stool in the hall and takes up her address book. She finds June's number and dials.

'Hello, June? Is that you? It's Mrs Poll here, Kitty Poll. How is your father dear?'

Kitty listens and relaxes a little when she hears that Bert is frail, but still as sharp as a new pin.

'I thought I might come and see him.' Kitty speaks carefully and clearly into the telephone.

She waits, listening and staring down at the calendar that she has brought with her from the kitchen.

'Yes, dear, yes – Tuesday will be fine.' She reaches for a pen and writes down Bert's name. 'June, can you tell your father that I've had a letter from Sammy Ray Bailey's grandson in America. He wants – Sammy Ray Bailey, yes dear yes, your father will know who he is – he wants to know about the war. Okay then, dear – I'll see you on Tuesday.'

Kitty takes the calendar back to the kitchen and hangs it on the nail in the pantry door. Yes, she thinks, this is the right thing to do. Bert will know what to tell Sammy's grandson. For a moment she considers Sammy as a grandfather, but the thought does not crystallise. In her mind she sees him as he was back then, the day he brought the bicycle back.

May 1944

Kitty had fallen from the bicycle on Tuesday evening and by Saturday morning her knees had hardened into dark-red scabs. She stood in front of the full-length mirror, holding up her skirt while Dora and Gwendolyn peered over her shoulders and studied her reflection.

'It's not too bad, chick,' said Gwen. 'Skirt lengths are shorter but we'll still cover those knees up.'

Gwendolyn took up the paper parcel that Kitty had brought with her. Aunt Vi had given her two old dresses for Gwendolyn to refashion. Though the dresses no longer fitted Aunt Vi, they were much too big for Kitty. Dora giggled as Gwendolyn held them up.

'Don't laugh, Dee, darling, this lemon is gorgeous material – it'll look lovely against your dark hair, Kitty. And it's good that there's plenty of it and so little of you – if I cut it right, you'll get a dress and a little jacket to cover your shoulders.'

She placed it on the bed and shook out a long grey dress and pulled a face. 'Cor, this one's not much fun, is it? Still, we'll get you a nice skirt or two out of it.' Gwendolyn turned her attention to Dora. 'So, what have you got, sis?'

Dora's face fell. 'I thought you were bringing something . . .' Her voice trailed away. Gwendolyn went to a case that was placed on a chair beside the bed.

'Something like this you mean?' she said, holding up a blue coat dress.

'Oh Gwen, Gwennie it's lovely!' Dora squealed.

'Well, it's got a bit tight on me – I reckon I'm the only girl in London getting fat on rations! It'll look lovely on you, Dor – we'll add a dark-blue trim on the cuffs and pockets. I'll show you how to do it.'

Gwendolyn went downstairs to fetch the sewing

machine and, while she was gone, Kitty told Dora about Sammy finding her after the accident. Dora was beside herself with excitement.

'Are you going to see him again?' she asked.

'See who again?' Gwen asked, returning to the bedroom and lifting the sewing machine on to a writing desk in the window.

'Kitty has an American pilot!' said Dora before Kitty could speak.

Kitty laughed and blushed. 'What she means is that an American pilot found me – when I fell off my brother's bicycle. He helped me home.'

'Sounds like Dora's right for once,' Gwendolyn said, smiling. 'I'm sure you have got him, Kitty – smart move throwing yourself at his feet!'

'Oh, but I didn't, I mean he hadn't arrived when – I had no idea he was there!'

Gwendolyn laughed. 'I'm only teasing you, you know.'

'I looked like a scarecrow and my knees were bleeding.' Kitty shuddered at the memory.

'You're so lucky,' sighed Dora. 'An American pilot. I'd give anything to be rescued by an American pilot! What's his name?'

'Sammy Ray Bailey,' Kitty said and couldn't help smiling when she said it.

'Oh, it's such a wonderful name! Isn't that a wonderful name, Gwennie? Is he handsome?'

Before Kitty could reply, Gwendolyn took her by the shoulders and sat her down at the dressing table.

'Right, Kitty, if your young man isn't smitten, he soon will be. Now, let's look at you. You've got lovely hair, look how it curls – now that's what I'd give anything for.' Then to her sister she said, 'Don't be daft, Dora, of course he'll be handsome, I've not met one yet who isn't.' Gwen picked up her hairbrush and began brushing Kitty's hair.

'He'll be able to get you nylons – be sure to ask him, they get ever so much money, so he won't mind. They really know how to have a good time the American boys do – they like to take a girl dancing, treat her right.'

Dora wandered over to her sister's bed and picked up a pair of stockings and let them trail through her fingers.

'Did an American give you these, Gwen?'

Gwendolyn glanced over her shoulder and Kitty grimaced as she accidentally tugged at her hair.

'Don't you go snagging them, Dor! Well, yes as it happens, they were a present from an admirer.' Gwendolyn laughed at the younger girls who both stared expectantly at her. 'Ooh, aren't you a right nosey pair!'

Kitty studied herself in the mirror while Gwen styled her hair, rolling it back at her brow and temples and fixing it in place with hairpins. She could see that it made her look older and she lengthened her neck and held her head carefully. It was a strange feeling, as if her own face were no longer familiar to her and she were looking at someone else. When Gwen announced that she had finished, Kitty thanked her and moved out of the chair so that Dora could take her place.

Kitty sat on the edge of the bed and listened while the sisters chattered. She stole quick glimpses of herself in the mirror and decided that she liked her new hairstyle, and she even dared to think that she was pretty. When she thought about Sammy seeing her like this, she felt a wave of happiness and anticipation, but a sinking feeling of dismay quickly followed it. He had noticed her because she was hurt and crying and lying in the road beside a broken bicycle. She did not dare to imagine that he would have shown any interest in her otherwise.

And what did she know of proper grown-up relationships between men and women? She could not see herself being taken to a dance hall and nor could she imagine ever asking Sammy to buy her stockings. She watched Gwendolyn's beautiful face as she teased Dora and felt certain beyond doubt that Sammy would prefer a glamorous girl like Gwendolyn to a choir girl with scabs on her knees.

On Sunday, Kitty dressed carefully in her new dress and rolled and pinned her hair the way Gwendolyn had done it. She watched from her bedroom window and when she saw Sammy turn the corner, she ran downstairs and went out to meet him. But when she reached the gate, there was no sign of him. He must have stopped, or worse, turned heel and gone away. Kitty wished herself back indoors but couldn't move; she was rooted to the ground by a mixture of embarrassment and disappointment. Then suddenly, there he was and Kitty lurched forward, any possibility of behaving naturally now completely lost to her. She reached for the latch at the same time as him and there was an awkward moment as they worked out who should open it. As Sammy's hand brushed against her fingers, Kitty felt the sensation of his touch to be shockingly exaggerated. For some reason, she heard Gwendolyn's voice in her head. *Smitten – he'll be smitten!* Kitty blushed scarlet and lowered her head.

'Do come in.' Her voice struck her own ears as impossibly pompous. *Do come in! Do come in?!* Who did she think she was? The Queen?

Aunt Vi stood at the open door smiling, her apron dusty with flour.

'Come on, Kitty, bring the young man inside for his tea, don't keep him standing in the garden!'

'How're your knees?' Sammy asked, then immediately regretted it when he saw Kitty's face flushed with embarrassment.

He ducked though the doorway behind Kitty and followed her into a small room where the table was laid for tea. Sammy glanced at it – homemade biscuits, a loaf of bread, some cheese and a cake. He guessed they didn't always eat a tea like this. Hovering over the table was a teenage boy who looked like he would happily scoff the lot.

Sammy held out his hand.

'You must be Charlie – pleased to meet you.'

Charlie extended his hand slowly and, after quickly scanning the uniform, he stared hard at the serviceman's face. This was the first American that he had seen close up. His main experience was from the cinema and this specimen was disappointing – no suntanned swagger, no chiselled features; nothing at all to suggest a hero. He was not especially tall, his hair was mid-brown and his eyes were more of a non-colour than anything that might catch your attention. His complexion was pale and he had dark circles beneath his eyes. There was nothing that told Charlie that he was in the presence of a fighter pilot. In fact this lean young man was barely more grown-up than Charlie was himself.

Yet, once he had hold of Charlie's hand, the American grinned and a pair of creases ran in curves, from the corners of his eyes to the widely drawn edges of his mouth. Charlie smiled back.

'I have something that belongs to you outside. D'you wanna come and see what you think?' Sammy gestured towards the front of the house with a nod of his head.

'My bicycle?' Charlie's voice faltered and he flashed Kitty a quick look. 'Is it all right?'

'I've got the kettle on,' Aunt Vi called from the kitchen as they moved to leave the house. 'Uncle Geoff will be home in a minute and then we'll have our tea, so don't you be long out there.'

Once outside, Sammy strode up the path and out the gate followed by Charlie and then Kitty. He reached the rowan tree that had been allowed to grow through the hedge. Propped against it was Charlie's bicycle and Kitty understood why it had taken longer than she had expected for him to arrive at the gate.

With his back to them, Sammy took hold of the saddle and handlebars and lifted the bicycle round and placed it in front of Charlie as if he were presenting him with a prize.

'I know the colour's not right but it's all I could find,' Sammy said. 'It's what's used on the Spitfires if they need touching up.'

'Spitfires,' Charlie repeated. 'Spitfires? Oh my gosh, oh my gosh! Spitfires!'

He took hold of the bicycle, swung himself on to the saddle and pedalled away down the road.

Sammy laughed. 'Well, he seems pleased with it.' He turned to Kitty. 'Looks like he won't kill you after all.'

Kitty thanked him and smiled back. They stood in front of each other smiling, while Kitty thought to herself, *Say something else, stop staring like a fool and say something* – but she could do nothing but hold his gaze and smile. Charlie came cycling towards them, his arms out like wings, and they laughed.

They returned to the gate and met Uncle Geoff coming the other way. Charlie had dismounted and was inspecting the stripes of white paint that now adorned his mudguards.

'So you can be seen at night,' Sammy said, 'in the blackout.'

'Charlie's only fifteen – we don't let him ride about at night,' Uncle Geoff said quietly.

'No sir, I only thought – you know, maybe in wintertime for when it's darker.'

Sammy stood straight and gave the older man his full attention. Kitty held her breath. She desperately wanted Uncle Geoff to like him.

'Well, maybe he won't need them come the winter,' Uncle Geoff said. 'Now that we have the help of the

United States Army, this war will be over by Christmas – isn't that what people are saying?'

'Sammy joined up as soon as he was old enough – he's been here since '41,' Kitty said. Uncle Geoff looked at her and away again.

'Look,' Charlie said, wheeling the bicycle towards his uncle. 'Sammy's painted the frame with Spitfire paint.'

'Has he now?' said Uncle Geoff, glancing down at the bicycle then back at Sammy. 'I wouldn't have thought the Air Force had paint to spare for boys' bicycles.'

Kitty's heart sank; she could see no hope for Sammy now.

'Well, no sir, you're absolutely right – it hasn't. I waited for the ground crew to finish a repair and I kind of worked the brush clean on Charlie's bicycle.'

There was a pause and Uncle Geoff nodded and held out his hand.

'Mr Bellamy.'

'Samuel Bailey, sir – pleased to make your acquaintance.'

Aunt Vi called them in for tea and Kitty stole an admiring glance at Sammy – it might be too soon to say, but it seemed to her as though he had just achieved the impossible and won round Uncle Geoff. He caught her looking at him and smiled.

The next time Kitty saw Sammy was the following Tuesday evening at a Welcome Committee Concert organised by Mrs Parkes and Reverend Howles at the request of the American Red Cross. It was due to start at seven o'clock, but Kitty arrived at the village hall at six-thirty with the other members of the choir for a last rehearsal. After they had climbed the steps to the stage and found their places, Mrs Parkes told them what an important job they were doing. Kitty stared intently at Mrs Parkes and tried to stand up straight while Dora jabbed her in the ribs with her elbow.

'These young men are just like your fathers, brothers and sons – they are a long way from home and no doubt missing their families very much. It's important that we share with them our values and standards and show them some decent society.'

Kitty knew that Mrs Parkes was shocked that some of the town girls had been seen walking out with American soldiers, because she had overheard her talking to Auntie Vi about it. 'Consorting,' she had called it.

They were singing 'Linden Lea' for the second time when the door opened and Sammy stepped into the hall.

Kitty could be relied upon to carry the melody with confidence, and so Mrs Parkes glanced up from the piano when she heard her falter. Sammy raised a hand in apology and retreated backwards through the open door. The gesture had been aimed at Mrs Parkes and the vicar, standing beside her as page turner, but somehow Sammy had managed to catch Kitty's eye and smile at her. As the door closed behind him, a wave of murmured interest spread through the choir and Dora turned to Kitty and raised her eyebrows.

'Ladies, please, ladies!' Mrs Parkes called sharply. 'We haven't much time. Let's run through it once more, if you please!'

She adjusted her music, flapping away the vicar's hands as he tried to assist her before adding, 'And will you kindly concentrate, Kitty Danby!'

Kitty's mind was overwhelmed by the intensity of

her feelings. So much so that she felt disconnected from what was happening around her. She didn't take in a word of the vicar's lengthy welcome speech. And the musical recitals, the singing, serving tea and making polite conversation to khaki-clad Americans passed by with Kitty not noticing anything but her own state of excitement. She kept reliving the happy shock of seeing Sammy smiling at her from the doorway. The hall was crowded and they spoke only briefly, but in Kitty's memory of that night it was as though she and Sammy had been the only two people there.

Each time she looked across the hall, she found him immediately, and no sooner had her eyes rested on him than he had looked away from the person he was addressing and their eyes met. Similarly each time she glanced away from the face before her, it would be to find Sammy looking at her.

When it was over, Aunt Vi had the job of washing up the cups and saucers and tidying the hall and Kitty helped her. By the time they left, dusk was falling. It had been hot inside and as they stepped out into the chill air, Aunt Vi paused to put on her cardigan.

'Well, you sang beautifully, Kitty dear, as usual. I shall write and tell your mum all about it in my next letter – she would have loved to have heard you, my word, she would.'

Most people had dispersed, but a small group of airmen stood to one side of the door talking and laughing. Sammy was with them and he turned towards them, still grinning from the shared joke. He spoke to Aunt Vi.

'Ma'am, I'd like to walk you and Kitty home, if I may.'

Before she could reply Charlie rode up on his bicycle and screeched to a stop beside them.

'Ah, here's my chaperone,' said Aunt Vi, 'but I daresay that Kitty will be glad of the company, Sammy.'

As they set off for home, Charlie dismounted and, wheeling his bicycle beside him, he fell into step with Sammy.

'Our mum drives an ambulance in London,' he said.

'Kitty didn't tell me that,' Sammy replied, turning towards Kitty and smiling broadly. Charlie dropped back, moved behind Sammy then sped up on his other side, pushing his front wheel between Sammy and his sister.

'She used to work in munitions but now she's a driver. I can't wait till I drive. What's it like flying a Spitfire?' he asked.

'Well, it's great. I mostly fly a Mustang now,' Sammy said, reluctantly turning his attention from sister to brother.

'Won't you tell me what it's like though?' Charlie persisted.

Aunt Vi shook her head. 'Come on, Charlie, let's you and I go on ahead and leave Kitty and Sammy to get to know each other a bit.' Then to Sammy she said, 'Will you join us again for Sunday dinner – you can satisfy this boy's curiosity then.'

Flying schedule permitting, Sammy accepted and Aunt Vi shooed Charlie away. Kitty and Sammy walked on in silence for a few minutes until the shadowy figures of Aunt Vi and Charlie, wheeling his bicycle beside her, disappeared in the gloom.

'You know, I shouldn't be here by rights,' Sammy said at last, 'in Kent, I mean. I made an emergency landing a few weeks ago – I'm still getting fixed up.'

'Oh,' said Kitty. 'Were you hurt?'

Sammy shook his head and laughed. 'No, I'm fine – it's my plane that took it bad. It was going to be my last flight for a while – I was due R and R after that – you know? Rest and recuperation? But now I've volunteered for something that means I have to stay here a while.'

'Do you think you'll be able to come on Sunday?' Kitty asked.

'I hope so – but I was wondering if I could see you sooner than that.'

Kitty felt her insides tipping over.

Sammy went on. 'This will maybe sound like a mean thing to say but I sure am glad that you fell off that bike.'

Kitty laughed. 'Yes, well I'm glad that you came along and found me – though I'm not glad that you made an emergency landing – I don't like the sound of that.'

Sammy stopped walking and touched his fingers against her elbow. 'It was kinda hair-raising – I never thought that I wasn't gonna make it, but it was a close thing.'

'Sometimes we hear engines spluttering out and I always try to imagine the pilot inside, and hope that somehow he knows that I'm wishing him safely down.'

Sammy imagined how it might be to fly a mission having this girl willing him home and he suddenly understood what had been intriguing him and drawing him to her. Talking to her was as easy as thinking.

'I flew over your house the day after I found you. I was test-flying a Spitfire and I wanted to have a look at your place from the sky.'

Kitty thought, *He flew over my house.* She said, 'I'd love to see that.'

'Well, actually, I was hoping to see you.'

'And did you?' Kitty caught her breath and tried to remember.

'No, I saw your uncle working in the garden but you were nowhere to be seen.'

'I would have waved,' Kitty said. It was too dark to see his face properly, but she could feel his attention on her and the warmth in his hand. Sammy's fingers slid down her arm and found her hand and they walked on.

'So, can I see you tomorrow? It'll be around nine by the time I get free. It's kind of late – do you think it'll be okay?'

'Yes, I should think it would be all right.' Kitty felt

certain that Aunt Vi would be pleased to see Sammy; she could imagine her plumping up the cushions for him and offering him a cup of Ovaltine. But she was not sure that Uncle Geoff would welcome him.

'I'll tell Aunt Vi to expect you,' she said, secretly hoping that it would be one of Uncle Geoff's nights to meet Tom Farrell for a drink at the pub.

They continued to dawdle home. Kitty listened carefully as Sammy described the home farm where his mother made cakes that he called snow buns because they melted in the mouth. He asked her about London. Kitty told him how she felt as if her life were on hold until the war was over.

'When I left the school here I wanted to go home and do a secretarial course, but my mum won't have either of us coming back to London until the war's over. So I help Aunt Vi and I volunteer for war work locally. Charlie's been doing farm labouring, but what he really wants to do is fight the Nazis.'

'Your mother is right – you've gotta stay right here,' Sammy said, 'and Charlie's not going anywhere either – this war will be over long before he's old enough to fight in it.'

When they reached the house, they paused by the

rowan tree where, unseen by anyone who might have been watching out for them, they kissed. It was sweet and simple that first kiss: a brief touching of lips. Kitty went inside and called out a goodnight and climbed the stairs to her room. *Dear me*, she thought as she closed her bedroom door and leaned against it, *I've fallen in love*.

August 2006

Kitty reverses out of the carport that stands on what was once Uncle Geoff's vegetable patch. A horn blares from a passing car and Kitty jumps and hits the brake hard. *People drive far too fast round the lanes*, she thinks. *You wouldn't want to walk along them at night these days; you would be risking your life.* Kitty drives to Maidstone and parks at June's house. June comes to the door with a can of furniture polish in one hand. She gives Kitty the key to her father's bungalow.

'Tell him I'll be round at six with his tea.'

Kitty leaves her car outside June's and walks down

the road to Bert's. She lets herself in and calls out to him. His voice reaches her from a back room and Kitty walks down the hall and through the kitchen to a sunroom where Bert is sitting in front of open patio doors.

'Ah, Kitty,' he says and leans forward in his chair.

Bert's eyes are watery and blue. Brilliant white tufts of hair sprout from a mostly bald head. Once a big man, he is now thin. His shoulders, collar bone, hips, elbows, wrists and knees, the points which used to connect toned flesh and muscle, now protrude through his clothes.

'Hello, Bert dear. How are you feeling?'

'Mustn't grumble,' he replies and begins to cough. The coughing lasts a minute and leaves him breathless. Kitty takes the letter from her handbag and passes it to Bert, then she goes to the kitchen to make them some tea. She calls back as she leaves the sunroom. 'Just think – I would never have got it, if I hadn't taken on Vi and Geoff's old place.'

Kitty returns with the tea and waits while Bert finishes reading the letter. He holds a magnifying glass over the sheet of paper. His lips move as he reads.

'I suppose he's dead, then? This lad'll be wishing

he had been interested in the war when his grandad was still alive.'

'They're so busy with their own lives these days,' Kitty says.

'Huh!' Bert pulls a face then returns his attention to the letter. 'He'd have been well into his eighties now. I'm ninety-three next month.'

'He'd be eighty-two,' Kitty says. 'He was four years older than me.'

'He flew a Mustang P-51.'

'Yes.' Kitty passes Bert a mug of tea. 'I thought that you would know better than me the sorts of things this young grandson of his would like to know.'

Bert nods his head and lifts the wavering mug to his lips. He blows across the surface of the tea before sucking in a mouthful.

'He was a nice lad, yes, he was – no swagger about him like some of them.' Bert leans towards Kitty as if he is confiding a secret. 'He was a bloody good pilot too, in those cockpits for up to six hours at a time they were on those escort missions. Bombing the German factories you see, Kitty, leading up to D-Day. Muck up Nazi plane production. Keep the

Luftwaffe out of the skies. The P-51s were fast – they put Rolls Royce engines in them.' Bert's eyes shine and he smiles at Kitty. 'Not as quick to turn as the Spits to my mind, but they were fast, blow me they were. And they could go the distance.' He nods his head, agreeing with himself.

Kitty puts her tea down and pulls her handbag on to her lap.

'I've brought a pen and notebook Bert, hang on a second, I'll write it all down.'

May 1944

Bert had finished a last check of the guns when Sammy approached and climbed on to the left wing of the Mustang. He liked this boy's ease with the machine. You could see that Sammy didn't feel claustrophobic inside the cockpit. In fact, he looked as though he would like to pull everything in closer if he could. Bert watched as Sammy stowed the survival kits before stepping into his shell. He wriggled about in the seat settling into the familiarity of the space. He adjusted the rudder pedals and passed his arms through the shoulder harness, briefly reaching down to pat the inflatable dinghy and slide his hand over the survival pack. He raised the left-side panel of the perspex cockpit enclosure then lowered the upper portion. He secured the pins and made sure the handle was locked in place and that the felt moulding on the seals was in position. He grinned at Bert and gave him a thumbs-up before beginning the pre-flight procedure.

There was a sign in the cockpit that said *Do not exceed air speed of 500 mph* and before every take off Sammy kissed the tips of his fingers and pressed them on to the sign for luck. Sammy radioed his readiness and waited, while in the field around him, the engines of other planes roared into life. Sammy checked the rendezvous times he had scribbled on the back of his hand, then glanced at his watch. Right on cue he received the order he was expecting from his flight leader.

'Red Two, this is Red Leader. Prepare to taxi for take off. Over.'

Sammy snaked his way up the field followed by his roommate, Mike, who was flying Red Three. At fifteen seconds past the minute, the two Mustangs took off into the pre-dawn sky. At thirty seconds past they were followed by two more. When the whole of Red

Group was airborne they pulled the Mustangs into their flight formation and set a course for Germany. They looked like a flock of mechanical geese.

As the fighters climbed, Mike began to sing, his voice ethereal in the headset. Sammy grinned, wondering how long it would take before Red Leader told him to shut up.

'Keep on doing what you're doin',
your love is driving me to ruin,
keep on doin' what you're doin',
'cos I love what you do to me . . .'

Mike sang on, his voice as light and happy as if they were heading out for a day at the beach. He got through the chorus and an entire verse of the Benny Goodman tune before Red Leader intervened.

'Put a sock in it, Red Three.'

'Oh shucks, sir, don't you love me any more?' Mike whined. 'What about you, Red Two? You love me, don't you?'

'Sorry to break it to you like this,' Sammy replied, 'but I've fallen in love with a girl called Kitty Danby.'

'Son of a gun!' Mike exclaimed.

'Okay, quit goofin' around! This is Red Leader establishing radio silence.'

Sammy's gut clenched with the first sensation of fear the instant they had crossed the English Channel and entered a drift of thin cloud over the coast. Deeper into Germany and Sammy's fear heightened a degree or two as the minutes passed. Fear was such a familiar feeling to him now that he found it tolerable. He was checking the sky; over his left shoulder, to the left, in front, to the right and over his right shoulder – his head moving in a continuous sweep.

They had reached the rendezvous and were flying at twenty-thousand feet when they saw the B-24s a few thousand feet below them. These were the bomber planes they had come to escort and protect from enemy fighter-fire. They were heavy and slow and vulnerable to the German fighter planes, the Messerschmitt 109s, launched to stop the bombers reaching their destination.

Suddenly, radio silence was broken with the code to tell them that enemy aircraft had been sighted. 'Bandits at six o'clock, bandits at six o'clock. Over.'

'This is Red Leader, we've got two 109s at six o'clock, low. In you go, Red Two, take your wing-man. Good luck. Over.'

Sammy jettisoned the reserve fuel tank, then set his sights on the Messerschmitts and dived. A quick glance over his shoulder told him that Mike was with him. They had barely closed the gap when the enemy planes parted and dived. Sammy radioed Mike.

'Red Three, this is Red Two, I'll take the left. Over.'

'I'm on it. Over.'

As his plane plummeted, Sammy began shouting over the noise of the engine. He yelled out incomplete sentences; a mixture of coaxing and swearing. His brow was tightly furrowed, his knuckles white, he reminded himself to breathe. He felt the pressure in his head and the buzz through his feet as the engine's work increased. He pulled back and decelerated. Coming through the cloud and sitting just below it, he scanned the sky for the enemy plane.

Another huge wave of fear coursed through him as he took in the empty sky. Where was it? He was extra cautious for a minute or two, varying his height and speed, but there was no sign of it. He increased altitude and regained radio contact with Red Leader.

'This is Red Two, do you read, over?'

'Copy that, Red Two. You got Red Three with you?'

'He went after one 109 – I took the other.'

'Okay, Red Two. Red Three, Red Three do you copy? Come in, Red Three.'

Bert watched on as Sammy and a couple of the others waited beside the hut that the ground crew used as a tool store. Their faces were as grey as the sky and streaked with grime. Time passed and reason told them that Mike wasn't coming back. One of the bomber crews said that they had seen a Messerschmitt 109 pursuing Mike into cloud after he had broken away from the escort party. No one had seen him after that. It was possible that he had made an emergency landing somewhere else. They didn't discuss it; they just waited.

Bert had a primus stove in the hut and he passed black sweet tea to the waiting pilots. They knew that it was a pointless wait, but they were reluctant to leave. Eventually, they finished their tea, lit their cigarettes and wandered back to the mess for the debriefing. No one said a word. Later it was confirmed that Mike's plane had been hit and he hadn't bailed out.

Sammy was hanging about putting off going to his bed, doubtful that he would be able to sleep, when he was given a message that his commanding officer wanted to see him. Sammy knocked and entered the small office. Apparently, Mike had left a note in his locker saying that he wanted Sammy to have his books. Sammy took the books, all of them poetry collections, and went to the room he had shared with Mike. Someone had already been in and cleared away Mike's things.

Sammy placed the books back on the shelf where Mike had kept them. Then he took one volume up again and sat on his bed with the book in his lap. He didn't much care for poetry. He flicked through it for a while until he suddenly felt the wakefulness draining out of him. A heavy fatigue and the desire to sleep crept through his body like black ink seeping across blotting paper. Sammy let the book slide to the floor and lay down.

He woke from a bad dream around two in the afternoon. He was cold and his left arm was beneath his chest and numb. He heaved himself up and sat on the edge of his bed, nursing his lifeless hand. His blanket had fallen to the floor and, as he picked it up, he saw the book. He reached for it and turned it over in his hands. He read the spine, Robert Graves – what a name, no wonder he had had a nightmare.

Sammy stood and went to the window. The sky was grey and it was raining again. He dressed and, taking Mike's book, went out for some air. He crossed the airfield and stood for a while just inside the hangar, straining his eyes to read in the gloom. He thumbed through the pages scanning the first lines until he found a short poem that he read in its entirety. It was called 'Love Without Hope'.

Love without hope, as when the young bird-catcher
Swept off his tall hat to the Squire's own daughter,
So let the imprisoned larks escape and fly
Singing about her head, as she rode by.

And suddenly he found himself thinking about Cory Weston. He saw her, clear as day, walking to school hugging her books to her chest – tall and straight and graceful, the morning sun catching her red hair. And he realised that he hadn't thought about Cory in a long time. And, remembering all of a sudden that he had once harboured the fantasy of going home a hero and marrying her, he shuddered. The idea of marrying Cory Weston seemed ridiculous to him.

Sammy had loved Cory all his life. He was the same age as Cory's little sister, Flick, and she adored Cory too. Together they followed her around like twin shadows. But Cory Weston barely knew that Sammy Ray Bailey existed.

Sammy found his wallet and took out the picture of Cory that he kept there. He stood for several minutes, sheltering from the English drizzle, studying Cory's face, trying to remember what it was that he had felt for this girl. And that's where Bert found him. Sammy was so engrossed that he jumped when Bert spoke to him.

'Is that your girl?'

Bert nodded at the photograph Sammy held against the open page of his book.

Sammy blushed to the roots of his hair and Bert laughed.

'She's a lovely-looking girl. I hope she waits for you, son.'

Sammy experienced an uncomfortable sensation, a mixture of embarrassment and shame as he imagined what Cory would do if she'd heard herself referred to as his girl. He had been carrying her photograph with him ever since he stole it from the Weston home five years before. It occurred to him now that, if anything happened to him, maybe someone would find the photo and give it to his parents and then everyone would know that he had been sweet on Cory. The thought appalled him.

He read the poem again and this time he saw the boy sweeping off his ludicrous hat and the birds escaping in a great noisy humiliating spectacle. All at once Sammy realised what a fool he had been. And he realised too that he was a completely different person from the boy who had had a secret love for Cory Weston.

He thought then of Kitty Danby and understood with a certainty that he had never felt before that she was the one; she was his future. Kitty, not Cory, was his reason for getting home alive.

He hesitated about what to do with the photograph and for a moment his hand curled round it as he considered screwing it up and throwing it away. But he could not do that. He reasoned that it wasn't Cory's fault that he didn't love her any more.

Instead, he decided that one day he would slip the photograph back in the dresser drawer in the Westons' kitchen. He didn't want to carry it on him any more so he put away his wallet and tucked the picture into the snug place where the page meets the spine and snapped the book closed.

Sammy ran after Bert and caught his arm. He had looked troubled when Bert had first seen him, and Bert knew he had plenty on his mind, but now he was laughing. Bert asked him what was so funny and Sammy told him that he was mistaken about the girl in the photograph. She had been a childish crush, he said, there had never been anything between them.

Then he went on to tell Bert about finding Kitty in the road and once he started talking he couldn't stop. He called her his little bicycle thief. He told Bert about her tears. He said he had heard the expression about being in floods and that he now knew it to be true. This girl nearly had them both standing in puddles. He described her prettiness, her gentleness, her beautiful voice. He had noticed her voice even while she was crying – it was not just the lilt of an accent strange to him, but a soft sweetness to her voice that drew him to her.

'That's the thing about her,' he told Bert, 'she's sweet and funny and pretty, but it just feels so right when I'm with her. She's the one for me, without a doubt, she's the one!'

August 2006

Bert reaches for his tea while Kitty sits and stares ahead. She has stopped writing.

'He fell for you, Kitty, that lad did – you were such a pretty little thing and he was over the moon about you.'

Kitty comes back to the present and smiles but shakes her head. 'No, you're wrong, Bert – he had a sweetheart back home.'

Bert waves his big bent hand dismissively.

'No, he told me that he was over —'

'I was very young and he wasn't much older . . . and the war, you know how things were, Bert.

People said a lot of things . . .'

Bert frowns, his lips move as if he is working himself up to speak, but he says no more.

'You're tired, Bert,' Kitty says as she notes his pallor and the loss of light in his eyes. 'We both are. I should be getting on now if I'm not going to get caught in the traffic.'

What Bert has told her about Sammy troubles her, but Kitty dampens her feelings by focusing her attention elsewhere. Bert seemed altered to her and she worries that remembering the war has been too much for him. She walks back up the road to her car and wonders whether she should tell June her concerns. She reaches the house and the sound of a vacuum cleaner from an upstairs bedroom window puts her off ringing the bell. June is busy and Bert, no doubt, will be fine after a rest. She drops the key through the letterbox.

Kitty drives home carefully. She tries not to think about what Bert has told her. The roads soon become busy. *There are bigger roads now*, thinks Kitty. There are dual carriageways and motorways and yet they still clog up. She remembers the lanes she walked as a young girl. *You hardly ever saw a car*, she thinks.

Then she remembers a time when Kent's lanes were full of traffic; a winding snake of vehicles that stretched for mile after mile.

June 1944

Kitty sat up in the darkness, her heart pounding.

'Who's there?' she said, her voice coming in a hoarse whisper.

'Look, Kit! Just come and look at this will you!'

Charlie was standing at the window beside her bed and the next moment he had it open and was leaning out. A loud drone filled the room: a magnified version of the sound that Kitty now realised had penetrated her sleep. She climbed out of bed and reached for her dressing gown.

'What time is it?'

'It's the invasion, Kitty!' Charlie grinned at her as

she squeezed beside him at the window. 'We're going to kick the Nazis out of France.'

The sky was beginning to lighten and in the shadows beneath the window, a convoy of mono-chrome vehicles rolled by.

'It's been going on for hours,' Charlie said. 'I was half asleep and I thought someone was out in a tractor. Then I realised that it had been going on too long.'

They heard shouts in the distance. Then a shouted order that came relaying towards them and in a moment or two the convoy came to a halt. In the semi-darkness, men began jumping from the backs of trucks, then spilling over the sides and suddenly there were men everywhere. Charlie whooped and ran across Kitty's bed in his haste to leave the room. Kitty got dressed and went down to the kitchen where she found Aunt Vi bustling around and pleased to see her.

Aunt Vi had the kettle and two saucepans on to boil. The enormous green enamel teapot was warming on the stove and she was placing cups on to a tray. A mixing bowl on the table stood beside the stone flour jar; one batch of scones was already waiting to go into the oven as soon as it was hot.

'Ah, Kitty,' she said, 'pop and fetch the willow, there's a good girl.'

Kitty hesitated.

'Hurry up, Kit, there's thirsty men out there and they'll not hang around all day.' She turned and poured the scalding water into the teapot and refilled the kettle from the tap. Kitty went to the dresser in the parlour and carefully took down the willow-pattern china teacups that Aunt Vi reserved for special occasions.

For the next hour, Kitty carried trays of steaming tea and plates of hot buttered scones out to the gate. She stood in the early morning light, smiling shyly, while a boisterous queue of soldiers downed the cups of sweet tea and helped themselves to half a scone. Kitty watched their hands as the cups were lifted full and lowered empty, rarely raising her eyes to see the faces of the men who thanked her. Occasionally, a 'Cheers, love' in a familiar London accent made her glance upward. When her tray was empty, she hurried back to the kitchen and Aunt Vi reloaded it. Uncle Geoff stood at the sink washing and drying the teacups, something that Kitty couldn't remember him ever doing before.

'Shall I do that, Uncle Geoff, and you can take the next tray out?' Kitty asked.

'You're all right, Kit,' he replied gruffly. 'I think they'd rather get their tea from a pretty girl than a dry old stick like me.'

Several soldiers asked her to marry them and, when a young Scot begged for a wee kiss, Aunt Vi, who had come out to the gate with another plate piled high with scones, teased him.

'It's a spanking not a kiss you'll get, you cheeky monkey!' A cheer went up from the men around them and the next proposal of marriage went to Aunt Vi.

More shouts from up ahead and the soldiers began to disperse. A few last men hurried up and took what was left on the tray and one, a wiry Cumbrian, when he had drained his cup, passed it absently into Aunt Vi's hand and murmured a low 'Thanks, Mam.' Kitty noticed Aunt Vi's chin tremble at this and saw her bite her lip before wishing him good luck.

'Oh Kitty,' she said, turning to go inside, 'I pray to God to keep them safe, I do.'

Charlie had cycled down the line to see how long the convoy was. Soon after the army was on the move again, he came back carrying an American comic and a baseball magazine. He stood with Kitty and watched them pass.

'I wish I was going with them, Kitty.'

But Kitty didn't answer him. She was thinking about Sammy. What would happen to him now?

August 2006

At ten to six June lets herself into her father's bungalow.

'It's me, Dad!' She places the Tupperware box she carries in one hand on the hall table and closes the door behind her. 'Brought you a bit of fish pie – I'll heat it up for you. Do you want peas with it?'

As June moves through to the kitchen she hears a sound coming from the bedroom. She calls out to her father again, questioningly this time, and his muffled reply has her frightened. She thinks he has fallen and hurries to the bedroom.

'Dad, whatever's happened?' she asks, alarm in her

voice. June moves round the bed and sees Bert. He is down on one knee, waving his walking stick about beneath the bed. His breath comes in rasps and wheezes and, as June rushes towards him, he struggles to speak.

'There's a box . . . can't . . . reach the . . . blessed thing. You get it, Junie, please.'

He uses the stick as a prop and slowly heaves himself up from the floor and sinks on to the bed. June goes down on both knees, tips her head sideways to the floor and peers past his slippers across the shadowy carpet. She retrieves a black metal box that was once used for storing cine-film canisters and places it beside Bert on the bed.

'You still got my old school reports in there, Dad? I should take them and show Martin. See if I can get him to do something with himself, instead of lazing around all day.'

Bert opens the box and begins lifting out documents and placing them on the bed. June sees the reports and picks them up from the pile. Bert continues to look. He is upset but June does not notice yet. At last his fingers fall upon a letter and he takes it up and holds it against his chest. A spell of wheezing becomes a coughing fit, slow at first like a reluctant starter motor trying to bite, then it takes hold and the cough consumes him, brings tears to his blue eyes. He rocks backwards and forwards and clutches the letter to him. The sun, which has been creeping along the wall outside, suddenly streams in at the window and a brilliant shaft of golden light illuminates Bert, but not June. She looks at her father and sees his distress.

'Whatever is it, Dad? What's the matter?'

Bert leans forward, one hand on his stick, the other pushing down on the bed beside him.

'Help me back to my chair.'

June gets up and takes her father's arm and he rises shakily. He thrusts the stick in front of him and leans on it as he swings his leg forward from the hip. Back in the sunroom June helps him into his chair.

The letter shakes violently in Bert's hand as he holds it out towards June. It looks as though he is admonishing her with it.

'What is the matter, Dad?' June asks again and there is an edge to her voice, concern perhaps or irritation, it is not clear which. She waits, she has no choice, while Bert's rasping breath slowly quietens.

At last he says, 'I've done a terrible thing, June.'

'Oh now, I'm sure you haven't, Dad.' June sits beside him and reaches for the letter, but Bert pulls it to him.

'I have, June, I've done a terrible thing. You have to help me.' He shakes his head then looks down at the letter. 'It was for Kitty, you see – he asked me to give it to her. He loved her, June, he loved her. And she loved him, I know that now. She loved him – I saw it, saw it in her face just now. It broke her heart.'

'What, Dad? What is it that you're saying? Who are you talking about?'

'It was a mistake – I see that now. I've done a terrible thing.'

June 1944

Aunt Vi held the *Picture Post* towards the lamplight and peered through her spectacles.

'They wrote all about it last month – course I didn't pay too much attention to it then. But, now that our boys are back in France, it helps to know what they're going through. Like moving the city of Birmingham, that's what it says, imagine that.'

'Read it out, Auntie,' Kitty asked, not because she wanted to hear it, but because she would be able to daydream and watch the clock uninterrupted while her aunt was occupied. Aunt Vi shook the magazine free of its crease and settled back in her chair.

'Let me see . . . oh yes, listen to this. "*Something comparable to the City of Birmingham hasn't merely got to be shifted: it's got to be kept moving when it's on the other side . . . there will be no food to eat, no water to drink, no roads or railways to travel on . . .*" Good heavens, Kitty, imagine – all that going on in that awful weather? Those poor men. There weren't even any harbours – they took them over with them. Can you believe it, Kitty?'

Aunt Vi sighed and fell quiet. It was a few minutes before ten o'clock and twilight was falling. Kitty stood up and went to the window. The sky was dark blue and the wind threw a fine spray of rain against the glass.

'I'm going to put my coat on and go out for a little while.'

'At this time of night? And it's raining Kitty!'

'I'll not be long and it's hardly rain, more like drops of moisture in the air.'

Aunt Vi smiled and shook her head, shooing her away with a flap of the *Picture Post*. She guessed where Kitty was going and who she was going to meet.

Kitty put a scarf over her hair and tied it beneath

her chin. She put her gabardine over her shoulders and stepped out into the garden and ran the few yards to the gate. As she stepped out on to the road, Sammy turned the corner and she ran to meet him. Sammy placed his hands on either side of her face and grinned at her before pulling her towards him and kissing her.

'Every time I leave you I think that you can't really be so wonderful, and here you are, just look at you.' Sammy kissed her again. Then, placing his arm across her shoulders, they walked together up the lane away from the village.

'Dora came round today. She was fed up because her sister Gwendolyn sent word to say that she couldn't get home and didn't know when she next would. It's Dora's birthday at the weekend and she was hoping Gwen would be here for it.' Kitty talked on about Charlie and Aunt Vi and the letter that she had had from her mother, until she sensed something was not right and stopped mid-flow.

'You're quiet,' she said, finally slowing her pace. Sammy lifted a curled hand and gently brushed his knuckles against Kitty's cheek. Kitty walked on slowly, suddenly finding it difficult to lift her feet.

'Are you going away?' Her voice came in a small, frightened whisper.

'I'm not going to be able to see you for a while, kitten. I have a couple of days' leave and then I'll be gone.'

Kitty felt her stomach turn. A few minutes ago, waiting to meet him, she had felt giddy with happiness. Now, she felt sick with fear that she might never see him again. She didn't trust herself to speak. She began to shake her head and covered her face with her hands.

'Kitty? Kitty, please, listen to me . . .' His voice was gentle, apologetic. 'I don't want to leave you. It's hard enough saying goodnight to you.' He tried to pull her hands from her face, but she dipped her head and wouldn't look at him. He wrapped his arms around her and bent his head over hers. When he spoke his mouth was close to her ear.

'I don't have any right to ask you this. We only just met and, if the world wasn't so crazy and mixed up, then we'd be going for walks and picnics. I want to take you dancing – just a normal couple having fun. But everything is mixed up and crazy, Kit – and jeez, if it wasn't I would never have met you. The thing is

Kitty, what I'm trying to say is, I'm so glad that I've met you. I'd like you to be my girl – if you want to? If you can wait for me?'

Kitty lifted her face to his and though she was smiling, she began to cry uncontrollably. Sammy threw his head back and laughed.

'Oh-oh, now we're done for – Kitty Danby crying in the rain – quick, someone build an ark!'

He pulled her to him and held her tight.

'I love you, Kitty, and when this war is over I want to be with you all the time, I want to marry you – if you'll have me?'

August 2006

By the time she reaches home, Bert's words have
stirred memories that Kitty has not allowed herself
to have before.

*He fell for you Kitty . . . he was over the moon
about you.*

The neighbour calls across the fence as Kitty locks
her car.

'How are you, Mrs Poll? Hot again – we could do
with some rain.'

Kitty raises a hand and smiles and is thankful that
her glasses have darkened in the sun and her tears are
not visible. *What a silly old fool I am,* she thinks as

she lets herself in at the front door. *After all these years.* Kitty drops her keys on the hall stand and goes upstairs to the glass-fronted bookcase on the landing. She slides back the glass and takes out the anthology of Robert Graves. She carries it into her bedroom and sits on her bed. She lets the book fall open in her hands and it still finds that page. It is all she has of Sammy's now. She destroyed his letters the night she had agreed to marry Roy but she had not felt the need to be secretive about the book.

The photograph is still inside, tucked between the pages. She lifts it out and stares at it. *And this is the girl who became Sammy's wife,* she thinks. *This is the girl he went home and married.* Kitty reads the poem on the page where Sammy left the photograph all those years ago. It is a poem about hopeless love. About their hopeless love, so she had always thought. There was a war, there was tragedy and death and sadness, and they were young. All her adult life, Kitty has reasoned that their youth and the extreme circumstances of war threw her and Sammy together and that it had been infatuation, not love. She had convinced herself that it would not have lasted the cold light of peacetime and was best forgotten. She believed that he had made a promise to a girl back home and that, with the war over, he had come to his senses and kept his promise. Kitty had, she thought, come to terms with these things many years ago. But now, sixty-two years later, she sits on her bed and is in tune once more with her sixteen-year-old self.

Suddenly, it is not Roy Poll, her husband of forty years, whom she thinks about, despite their happy marriage. Something long lost to her has been reawakened and it is Sammy Ray Bailey that she misses. She reads the poem and the last line blurs as the tears come again. She closes the book and holds it against her. She rocks gently and allows herself to imagine how her life might have been.

June 1944

The bus was already crowded when Kitty and Sammy squeezed past the conductor. Packed against the other passengers in the aisle, Sammy held on to an overhead strap with one hand and Kitty with the other, resting his chin on the top of her head. A man Kitty couldn't see was telling a joke and began laughing loudly as soon as he finished it. A few nearby passengers joined in good-naturedly. A woman beside Kitty was recounting the latest invasion news to the elderly man beside her who nodded as he listened.

They got off the bus close to Ashford's market and

walked arm in arm towards the town centre. There was a short queue outside the photographic studio, four soldiers in uniform and two women dressed for the occasion, one in a dress coat, the other in a two-piece suit, both with hat and gloves.

'Hey, now here's an idea,' Sammy said, stopping behind the women and gently pulling Kitty into line beside him. 'Let's get our picture taken.'

Kitty wasn't sure.

'My gran told me never to have my photograph taken with a young man . . .' She stopped and blushed, remembering that what Gran had actually said was that couples photographed together before their marriage would never be wed. 'She's a bit superstitious though – silly really.'

'No, sounds like just the thing my grandmother would say. How about we just get our pictures taken separately; then I can take you with me when I go and you can keep me here with you. How's that sound?'

'I wish you were going to be here with me, Sammy.'

'It won't be for long, Kitty – I'm sure of it – once we push them out of France, it'll be over.'

A young mother, carrying her little boy on her hip,

joined the queue behind them. The child was not much more than a baby and he stared shyly at Kitty and hid his face in his mother's neck when Sammy spoke to him.

'We're getting our picture taken for Daddy, aren't we?' the young mother said, tipping her head to see her small son's face. 'Daddy's gone to France, hasn't he?'

'I bet your daddy's proud of you!' Kitty said as the child lifted his face from his mother's shoulder. 'What's his name?' she asked the mother.

'William, his dad's William too – well, Bill.' Hearing his name, the child turned his head and stared at his mother.

Ten minutes passed and they moved up to the shop door and, at last, stepped into the studio followed by the young mother and her son. The two women in their Sunday best were waiting in front of them. The air was heavy with the smell of chemicals and furniture polish. A soldier came out through a curtain behind an oak counter, and was followed by a tall thin woman who went with him to the door and spoke to the people who were still waiting on the pavement outside.

'Mr Wilson regrets that he will not be able to photograph everyone waiting today. We've been expecting a delivery this afternoon and I'm afraid we're nearly out. If you could come back tomorrow.'

The photographer's assistant stepped back into the shop, turned the sign in the window from *Open* to *Closed*, and invited the two women to follow her through the curtain into the studio. The young mother was beginning to look flustered, as she struggled to entertain her child who was now fidgeting and squealing a protest at being held for so long. He arched his back, then made a grab for his mother's hair and succeeded in pulling the rolled curl at her temple free from its hairgrips. At that moment, the assistant reappeared from the back of the shop.

'Mr Wilson says he is very sorry but he can only do one more now – on account of those ladies wanting separate portraits as well as being done together.' Her look suggested that, if she had her way, the two women would not be getting one photograph, let alone three.

Kitty and Sammy glanced at each other and then at the harassed young mother who could not hide her disappointment. Kitty smiled at her.

'Would you like to go next? We were just passing by – I mean, it does seem a pity, now that you've got this far with the little one, for you not to go in.'

The young woman's face lit up.

'Oh, are you sure? Only Bill's going to miss his first birthday and I . . . Oh thank you, thanks ever so much.'

She balanced William on her hip and struggled to open her handbag and take out her comb. Sammy reached out and took the baby from her.

'Hey, big fella, let your ma fix her hair.'

Sammy held the boy up at arm's length over his head and Kitty opened her eyes wide and cooed at him.

'Look at you, young William! Look how big you are!'

William's mother took a compact from her bag and hurriedly tidied her hair and reapplied her lipstick. Kitty stood close to Sammy as he held the boy, and laughed with him as the child's fat little fingers scratched at the silver winged badge above Sammy's chest pocket.

Sammy squeezed Kitty's hand as they left the shop. 'I don't need your photograph – I can see you whenever I close my eyes.'

*   *   *

Later they had lunch in the tearooms where they were served steaming-hot bowls of the dish of the day and tried to decide if it was a thin stew or a thick soup. Kitty drank tea, but Sammy ordered coffee and then shuddered as he swallowed each mouthful.

'Wait until you taste my ma's coffee,' he said. 'I'll ask her to bake us a walnut and maple syrup pie – you've got to try that. Ma's pie with a cup of strong hot coffee – oh boy, that's the best.'

'I thought you said that snow buns were the best,' Kitty teased.

'Well, yes that's correct, they are too.' Sammy grinned, pleased that she had remembered.

Kitty smiled at Sammy over the top of her cup. He met her gaze but he was no longer smiling. Kitty slid her hand across the table.

'Come on, Sammy, we're going to enjoy today, remember? Forget all our worries for just one day.'

'Yeah, you're right,' Sammy replied. 'I was just thinking, you know, what if we got married straight away – then we could spend all our time together. When I'm flying out of Europe I won't be able to see you anyway. If we're married, then you could go to the States. My folks are going to love you, Kitty, and they'll take good care of you. I don't know – is it a good idea, what do you think?'

Kitty thought. Various scenes – the consequences, both delicious and frightening to imagine, of a hasty marriage and sailing to America alone, vied for attention in her mind. She imagined meeting Sammy's parents, seeing his home and being among the things he cared about and the people he loved. Then she saw herself alone and so far away from him. She imagined saying goodbye to Charlie and the possibility of never seeing him or her mother or Aunt Vi again. She imagined the Atlantic crossing, the steel-grey ship and unfriendly seas.

'I'm sorry,' Sammy interrupted her reverie, 'that wasn't put in the most romantic way.'

'Oh it's not that, it was romantic – it's just that America is so far away. It's hard to explain but, even though you'll be in France or Italy and I'm in England, I think I'd still feel as though we were under the same sky. When I get up in the mornings, I'll think of you and it will be morning for you too, and I think I'll feel close to you because of that. Do you understand what I'm trying to say? Does that sound silly?'

'No, that's not silly at all – you know, Kitty, you say something that hasn't occurred to me before and I know exactly what you mean and I think that you're right. I guess, it's just that, when I think of home, it is so safe, there's plenty to eat. No fighting, no bombs – I want to think of you there, safe and away from this war.'

'We're not doing very well, are we?'

'What do you mean?'

'Not thinking about the things that worry us.'

Afterwards they wandered into the park. It no longer had railings, half the grass area was now given over to an air-raid shelter and the flower beds were planted with vegetables. They sat together on a bench and talked. An elderly woman passed with a cocker spaniel on a lead. Sammy told Kitty about the farm dogs and the little mongrel that he had found half dead as he walked to school one day. It was a sad story and, as he told it, Kitty leaned towards him and studied his face and imagined the scene: Sammy at ten years old, playing truant from school so that he could care for the injured puppy. She was relieved when he got to the happy ending and suddenly felt overwhelmed by a mixture of love and pride. Sammy returned her gaze for a moment then grinned broadly.

'Actually, you remind me of Skipper when you look at me like that,' he said and began to laugh.

'Hey!' Kitty protested and raised her arm as if to slap him, but he caught her hand and pulled it to his lips and kissed her fingers.

'I'm kidding. It nearly drives me crazy when you look at me like that. I love you so much, Kitty.' He kissed her.

They were interrupted by a sharp voice.

'Kitty Danby – is that you?'

They broke away from each other and Kitty jumped to her feet and found herself looking at Mrs Parkes. Sammy stood up slowly and nodded at the older woman.

'Hello, Mrs Parkes. How are you?' Kitty said and was then horrified to feel herself blushing.

'I am very well, Kitty,' Mrs Parkes replied coolly. 'Tell me, does your aunt know that you are in Ashford with this young man?'

Kitty felt furious and indignant to be asked such an impertinent question. How dare Mrs Parkes imply that she was doing anything improper?

'My aunt knows perfectly well where I am and who I am with.' Kitty's voice wavered with anger. She glared at Mrs Parkes defying her to treat her as anything less than the adult she considered herself to be.

'Mrs Parkes, isn't it?' Sammy said then, stepping forward and offering his hand. 'Perhaps you don't remember me? You must meet so many servicemen at the socials you organise. You're very highly thought of, you know, ma'am. All the officers at the base sing your praises; why, they say, if it wasn't for Mrs Parkes, what would we do with ourselves?'

Kitty gazed up at Sammy as he spoke and then turned her head slowly back towards Mrs Parkes as he finished. She smiled as Sammy took her arm.

'Well, you must excuse us now, Mrs Parkes, but Kitty and I are going to the cinema.'

'Good day to you, Mrs Parkes,' Kitty said.

Sammy led Kitty away and, when she glanced over her shoulder, Mrs Parkes was still standing on the path beside the bench.

'Will she get you into trouble with your aunt?' Sammy asked.

'How can she? We haven't done anything wrong!' Kitty replied crossly.

'Well, *I* know that, but she seems the type to stir up mischief if she can.'

Kitty leaned her cheek against Sammy's sleeve and squeezed his arm. 'Let's forget about her. I don't want anything to spoil today and I am certainly not going to worry about Mrs Parkes. What shall we do now?'

'Well, what do you say we catch a movie?' he asked.

'I'd love to – I wonder what's showing?'

'Who cares? I'll just be happy to sit beside you. And it'll be dark so I'll be able to kiss you as much as I like.'

'Oh, that's what you've got planned is it?'

'Well, the thought did just cross my mind.'

'Hmm. We'll just have to see about that – I'm a very respectable young lady, you know.'

August 2006

Kitty carries her portable typewriter in its grey case to the dining room table where she heaves it up and opens it. She sits down and passes a sheet of paper through the roller and begins to type.

Dear John F. Bailey Rowe,

I did indeed know your grandfather and he was the very best of men. He spent some of World War Two stationed at an airbase near my aunt and uncle's home where I had been evacuated with my brother during the Blitz in London. A few years ago, after my husband died, the cottage came on the market again and I bought it as I have very happy memories of living here despite the war. As you see, Danby was my maiden name and I doubt your letter would have found me if it were not for my moving back here.

The brief time that I knew your grandfather was very special and he is fondly remembered. Personally, I do not know much about the planes your grandfather flew but I am still in touch with Mr Albert Wright who was a member of the ground crew at the airbase. He remembers your grandfather very well and I am enclosing some information that Bert has given me about the Mustangs – P-51s – that he piloted. I believe that he was an exceptional pilot. I know that he was brave and flew many missions into Germany accompanying the B24s that bombed the Luftwaffe factories before D-Day in 1944.

When I next go to the post office I will send you a book of poetry that once belonged to your grandfather – there is a photograph inside that was his also.

Yours sincerely,
Mrs Katharine M. Poll nee Danby

Kitty pulls the paper through the typewriter and replaces it with a clean sheet on which she types up the notes that she took at Bert's house. She reads everything through and imagines Sammy's grandson, a freckled, fair-haired teenager, pouring over flight specifications and battle manoeuvres. She signs the letter then folds it into a blue airmail envelope and carefully copies out John Bailey Rowe's address.

Soon she will take it to post, but now Kitty sits with the letter in her hands and in a moment forgets the boy it is addressed to.

June 1944

In the flickering darkness of the cinema, Kitty's mind wandered from the images on the screen. She had known Sammy for such a short time, yet being with him did not feel new or awkward. Kitty marvelled at this for a while, her small hand held in his large one. Just a few weeks ago she had not heard of Sammy Ray Bailey and now, somehow, she felt more at ease and happier than she had ever felt before. She didn't feel at ease with, say, Uncle Geoff whom she had known all her life.

In the film two men, one fat and one thin, were trying to move a piano. Sammy laughed at their slapstick antics – a loud joyous explosion that lifted his feet from the floor and threw his head backwards. Kitty turned to him and grinned, her own laughter soft and bubbling in her throat. He kissed her, then another laugh, partly suppressed, burst from him. With the warmth of his breath on her face, Kitty felt a rush of energy and thought she would melt into her seat. Sammy hooked his arm around her neck and pulled her close to him. Kitty leaned against him and let her attention drift between the film and her thoughts. Waves of laughter filled the auditorium and she thought, *If there wasn't a war on, this is how it would always be.*

And, just as Kitty was conjuring up a world without the war, the low wail of the air-raid siren began and the film juddered to a halt. Sammy grabbed Kitty's hand and pulled her into the aisle even as she reached for her coat. The majority of the audience were now making their way up the auditorium towards the foyer. Sammy went against the queue of people and towards the stage and screen, weaving his way between people and pulling Kitty along behind him. They arrived at the fire exit and Sammy dropped Kitty's hand and hit the bars so that the doors swung open. Several people turned then and followed them on to the street. The siren had reached full pitch and volume now and, as it was sited on the town hall opposite where they stood, they felt the full impact of it.

'We'll go to the public shelter in the park,' Sammy shouted, and he took hold of Kitty's hand once more and hurried on, adding, 'Are you all right?'

Kitty nodded. But, as they ran up the road, they saw an ARP warden in a side street guiding people into the cellar beneath a public house. Sammy took Kitty over to him.

'Did you see anything, sir?' he asked.

The older man looked up and his gaze took in Sammy's uniform.

'Something went over a while back – didn't recognise what. Couple of our boys were after it.'

Sammy squinted up at the early evening sky before guiding Kitty down the cellar steps.

It was cold and dingy and they made their way across the stone floor, past kegs of beer to the far wall. About thirty people were already settling themselves on hessian-covered sandbags. Sammy took off his jacket and placed it around Kitty's shoulders. Some people were talking, but they stood quietly holding hands in the dark, waiting for the siren that sounded the all-clear.

It was a long wait and they missed the bus they had planned to catch. When they reached the bus stop there was no one around and the emergency timetable was difficult to read in the dimming light. Kitty was faintly worried that Aunt Vi would be wondering where she was, but knew that it could not be helped. She would explain and Aunt Vi would understand that they had been caught in a raid and had to take shelter. Nonetheless, Kitty felt uneasy.

'Are you tired?' Sammy asked.

Kitty smiled and took a small step closer to him. 'I've had a wonderful day, Sammy,' she said.

'Me too.'

A man approached them. He was wearing the uniform of the Home Guard and he saluted Sammy before nodding at Kitty.

'There'll be no more buses from here tonight. What's your destination?'

Kitty told him and the man pulled a notebook from his pocket and studied it as he rubbed at his moustache.

'There is transport leaving from Kelly Street – take you some of the way. You could see if they have room for you. Best be quick, mind.'

They followed his directions but, as they turned into the end of the street, they saw a large group of people.

'We'll never get on,' Kitty said.

'Wait here a second, Kit.' Sammy nodded towards a group of servicemen standing beside a tarpaulin-covered lorry. 'I'm going to speak to those guys – see if I can get us a lift.'

Kitty sank her hands into her pockets and watched Sammy walk away. She saw the other men turn towards him and gaze at him for a few moments. Something he said made them laugh and, for some reason she could not explain, seeing it made Kitty proud. *Everyone likes Sammy,* she thought. *Everyone can see what a good person he is.*

'We're in – we just have to be a bit cute about it,' Sammy whispered as he returned to her side. He laughed. 'Don't worry – trust me.' He led her across the road as a voice shouted, 'Sorry, folks, That's it – no more.'

Kitty glanced back to where people continued to

stand around the transport as if they thought better news might come if they waited. The engine started up and the crowd began to disperse. The soldiers climbed into the back of their lorry and it too pulled away from the kerb.

'Oh dear, what shall we do now?' Kitty asked.

'It's okay, come on!'

They turned a corner and Sammy let his grasp slip from her elbow to her hand and broke into a run, pulling her along with him. He grinned at her over his shoulder and Kitty laughed as her feet skimmed the pavement. Behind her she heard the roar of an accelerating engine and the first lorry passed them. Then the second thundered by, and Kitty saw the smiling faces of the group of soldiers each reaching a khaki-clad arm out towards her. The lorry's gears crunched and it began to slow. One man, grinning broadly, leaned right over the tailgate and held his hand out to Kitty. The lorry pulled over and stopped.

'Go on,' Sammy murmured, 'I'm right behind you.'

Kitty reached up and took the soldier's hand and was hauled upwards so that she made a weightless climb over the tailgate.

Inside the lorry, she hesitated and smiled and nodded a general greeting into the gloom, aware that many men sat or crouched in the dimness. It was only a moment before Sammy had clambered in beside her but she had time to feel alone and uncomfortable. She was breathless and suddenly shy. The lorry smelled of diesel fumes, damp tarpaulin and sweat. There were other smells too, something sweet – and beer. The nearest soldiers sat with their backs to the walls, hands clasped on their knees. She felt herself being stared at. One or two greeted her. Then, Sammy was beside her again and she found his hand and held it tight. Sammy managed to sit down, his back against the tailgate as the lorry pulled away. Kitty fell against him and he pulled her on to his lap and put his arm around her shoulders. She caught his eye and he held her gaze for the briefest of moments. His look told her that everything was and would be all right and she felt herself relax.

Kitty rested her chin on Sammy's shoulder and looked out of the back of the vehicle and watched the road fall away behind them. She watched the rows of houses and then, as they left the town, the deepening blue V of sky between the hedges and trees. The light was fading fast as they approached the first village and the lorry pulled up beside the green. Kitty felt a twinge of anxiety as she thought of Aunt Vi waiting up for them.

'We don't want to get out here, do we?' Sammy asked quietly.

There was a low murmuring from deep inside the transport and the sound of shifting feet.

'It's a long walk from here,' Kitty whispered. 'Are they going on to the next village?'

A voice began to complain in the darkness and was met by a rally of protests.

'Leave off, will you?'

'Come on, Tucker – move it!'

'Ahh – keep your hair on, Pop.'

'We haven't got all night, son – sort yourself out.'

'There's no budging her – what am I s'posed to do?'

Kitty thought she had misheard but then there was another voice in the darkness – a woman's, treacly and thick as if she were slowing down or just waking.

'I'm happy where I am – I'm in heaven I am.'

A man sniggered. The driver, impatient to be moving, revved the engine.

'Come on, Tucker, get her out of here.'

'Come on, girl, up you get – wakey wakey!'

In the vying for space and shifting of bodies that followed, Kitty, Sammy and four soldiers climbed down from the lorry. Kitty stood on the road and noticed that her shoes were pinching her toes, that she had a sore place on her back, between her shoulders, and that she was thirsty and getting a headache. She also felt a nagging anxiety and, even though she told herself that Aunt Vi would understand, she couldn't shrug the feeling off. She looked at Sammy, but he was staring up into the transport and frowning. As Kitty's eyes moved from his face, she noticed that one of the soldiers standing beside the truck was staring at her. The way he looked at her chilled her; it was not a look that required a response – she might as well have been an object in a glass case. She wanted to walk away but instead moved closer to Sammy. He was watching the bustling movement inside the truck.

The soldier called Tucker reached the tailgate. He had his arm around the waist of a woman who, though she was smiling, appeared to be asleep on her feet. Tucker let go of her and began to climb out and the woman swayed until another man put his arm around her shoulders and steadied her.

'Oooh!' The woman giggled and swung round into the soldier, pressing herself against his body.

'Come on – time to go home, love.' The soldier pushed her away, then bent to lift her up and heave her out of the lorry and into Tucker's arms. Kitty saw that her blouse buttons were misaligned and that her lipstick was smudged.

Tucker placed the woman on her feet, set his hands on her shoulders then took them away. He let his hands hover near her as if she were a house of cards he had just built and was willing not to topple. She swayed, then staggered a few steps. A man yelled from the lorry and a handbag was thrown out. The soldier who had been staring at Kitty caught it.

'Right then, love, you'll be all right,' Tucker said and turned away from her. He rubbed his palms together as he waited his turn to board the lorry behind the other men. Only the staring soldier and Kitty and Sammy stayed put and made no move to return to the vehicle. Sammy touched Tucker's shoulder.

'Aren't you going to see her home?'

Tucker turned and pulled a face at Sammy.

'She's all right, bud – what's it to you?'

Kitty watched the woman walking slowly away in a meandering curve that would take her on to the green and towards a duck pond.

'Leave her with me – I'll see to her.' The soldier who held the bag made to follow the woman across the grass. A voice from within the lorry called out, 'Yeah, you'll see to her all right!'

The words were followed by laughter. An ice-cold feeling of dread landed heavily in Kitty's stomach.

'No, wait!' she said, stepping forward. She took hold of the handbag. 'It's fine, I'll go with her.'

The soldier held on to the bag for a moment but, as Sammy stepped up behind Kitty, he let out a sigh and pushed the bag towards her.

'We'll walk her home,' Sammy said. 'It's on our way, right?'

'Yes,' Kitty said. 'It's fine.'

The driver revved the engine again then crunched it into gear. With a last look after the woman, the soldier swore under his breath and ran for the lorry. He managed to clamber in as it pulled away. Kitty and Sammy watched him go then turned back just in time to see the woman sink to her knees.

August 2006

Kitty sits shaking her head. She wonders what became of that woman. *A girl really,* she thinks, *can't have been much over twenty.* It is strange to be thinking of her now. She has not given her a moment's thought in over sixty years. Kitty stirs herself from the table and plans to walk out to the post. *This won't do,* she thinks, *daydreaming all day.* But as she collects her keys in the hall and sets out with her letter in her hand, the name of the girl in the lorry jumps into her mind and her thoughts return to that night in 1944.

June 1944

Her name, she told them, was Joyce. They helped her up, supported her between them and guided her back to the road. It was quite dark by then and the waning moon, though still more than three-quarters full, had not yet risen above the treetops.

'Where do you live?' Kitty asked.

'Had to go did he? My young man?'

Kitty and Sammy exchanged glances. Joyce pointed to where a row of small houses led towards a pub and began to sing: '*Kiss me goodnight, Sergeant Major – put me in my little wooden bed!*'

They made for the cottage at the end of the terrace

and, as they approached, a side door opened and they were just able to make out the face of an older woman in the shadows. Joyce had hung between them, allowing herself to be dragged along, singing and giggling. But now she pulled herself up straight and took her handbag from Kitty.

'Hello, Ma,' she said, scraping her heels loudly as she climbed the kerb. Sammy and Kitty followed and waited for her to go inside. Kitty smiled at the woman she presumed to be Joyce's mother, not knowing whether to expect to be thanked for bringing Joyce home or to be asked for an explanation. But the woman stared blank-faced and, as soon as Joyce had passed through the doorway, she shut the door on them without a word.

'Oh dear,' said Kitty.

Sammy took her arm and they walked away. 'I'm sorry, Kitty.'

'I hope she'll be all right.'

'I'm afraid we're gonna have to walk now.'

'Well, I didn't want to get back in that lorry so —'

'Oh God, no, I'm sorry, I am so sorry, Kitty.'

They reached the pub and Kitty stopped to sit for

– not completely, but just enough so that I felt safe again; until I got a sense that the sea would hold me. When we came out of the water, my hands and feet were as white as paper and wrinkled like prunes. I remember feeling very pleased with myself.'

Sammy had moved closer to her and they walked on, their sides touching, her arm about his waist, and his arm across her shoulders. He kissed her hair.

'That's a wonderful memory to have, Kitty. How old were you?'

Kitty thought. 'I was four. We were visiting Aunt Vi and Uncle Geoff and went to the seaside for the day. That was the last summer Dad was with us. He died when I was five.'

Sammy murmured his sympathy and asked her what had happened.

'His appendix burst and they couldn't help him.'

They took a few more steps in silence before she continued. 'And I can remember something that he said to me that day too. I remember it because he said that some people say that kittens can't swim and he said, "You can do anything you put your mind to." There are other things I can remember, but they're vague – just feelings really, more a sense of him than a specific memory. Things like his rolled-up shirt sleeves, and watching him shave – and I think I can remember him and my mum kissing in the garden.'

They stopped walking and turned towards each other and kissed then. They kissed and clung to each other for a long time, and Kitty lost herself in the pleasure of being held against Sammy's body and the desire that made kissing him the only thing that mattered and drove everything else from her mind. They stopped kissing at last and stood facing each other, foreheads touching, fingers entwined and gasping for breath. Slowly, Sammy let go of one of Kitty's hands and pulled the other to his lips and kissed her palm. Then he leaned down and retrieved her handbag that had fallen to the ground as they embraced.

Sammy kissed her mouth and took her hand and they continued to walk. Kitty spoke first.

'You didn't finish telling me about the cabin – you said that your mother and your aunt didn't want it to be for fishing.'

Sammy laughed. 'You're not kidding; we came back from swimming expecting them to be laying out the picnic only to find them hanging pretty curtains at the windows. You should have seen my pa's face! Anyhow, that was just the start. Now there's furniture – a cloth on the table, pictures on the walls and roses by the door.'

'It sounds beautiful.'

'It is. I just got a letter from Annie: she says that Hal and Ivy had their honeymoon at the cabin. We'll do that too, Kitty, what d'you say? Just you and me, the birds singing in the trees – the river running by outside.'

He talked on and, as Kitty listened and imagined, she knew with certainty that she could do anything, would go anywhere with Sammy beside her. She knew that she was young, but she had experienced loss and uncertainty in her life and she understood that she could never know for certain what lay ahead. And yet, on that walk, Kitty believed that she was seeing her future and she both wanted it and believed it would happen. As they walked along the lanes, moving from darkness into pools of moonlight then back into shadow, she imagined them taking another walk together. She believed that one day, when the war was over, she and Sammy would hold hands and stroll through sunshine across the fields to the cabin by the river.

For a long time, Kitty had been oblivious to the discomfort of her slightly too-small shoes but, as they climbed the steep hill that would bring them within minutes of home, she began to tire. There was a farm gate in the hedge leading to a field and just inside the gate there was a hay barn. Kitty knew it well; the land belonged to a neighbouring farmer, Uncle Geoff's friend Tom Farrell. She and Charlie had often played there when they had first come to live in Kent and sometimes she and Dora met there still and nestled amongst the bales of hay for a chat.

'Can we stop for a little while, Sammy? I need to sit down for a few minutes.'

'Sure, anything you say. You're not worried about getting back?'

'We won't stop for long – just for a minute. I have to take my shoes off.'

They climbed the gate into the field and Sammy followed Kitty along the wall of hay bales to where the store had been dismantled for use and a few single bales stood. It was known as High Field and with good reason. They could see down the slope of the field to the road and the village beyond. It was a clear night and the moon was bright enough to bathe the grass in a silver sheen. Kitty sat down on the edge of the nearest bale and all but disappeared in the shadows. She leaned forward, reaching out into the light as she undid the laces of her shoes. She slackened them off, letting one, then the other, fall to the ground. As soon as her feet were free she knew she had made a mistake and that it would be agony to push her raw toes back into the shoes. She winced and Sammy turned from where he had been moon gazing and went to where she sat. He caught hold of her bare foot and gently pulled it towards him out of the shadow of the barn roof and into the moonlight.

'Hey, Kitty,' he said softly, 'you're bleeding.'

Kitty mumbled that she hadn't noticed and that it didn't really hurt. She felt her embarrassment burn her cheeks. For a second, she worried what he thought of her, but he took her face in his hands and kissed her.

'I'm sorry Kitty, I shouldn't have let you walk all this way.'

As she replied, he kissed her again and her words were muffled against his mouth.

'It's not your fault,' she repeated as Sammy let go

of her. He sat beside her and leaned forward to unlace his boots.

'What are you doing?' she asked then.

'I'm going to give you my socks – you can't put your shoes back on without socks.'

He kicked off one of his boots and started unlacing the other. He yanked off his sock, held it under his nose for a moment, shrugged and passed it to Kitty who squealed. Her eyes were wide,

'I won't get my shoes back on over your socks!' she said, laughing.

'Then you can wear my boots as well,' he replied. He had both socks off now and he stuck his bare feet out into the moonlight beside Kitty's.

'But what will you do?' she asked.

Sammy looked down at their feet. 'I will go barefoot.'

He spoke slowly and carefully and somehow his words changed the quality of the moment. Kitty stopped laughing and held her breath. He was sitting so close to her that, from her shoulder to her knee, there was no space between them. Kitty followed his gaze. Slowly, Sammy hooked his foot beneath Kitty's heel and raised her leg so that her foot rested on top of his. He sighed and shook his head.

'Oh Kitty . . .'

A sudden creep of shadow loomed across the grass towards them. Kitty looked up and saw Uncle Geoff standing a few feet away. He turned his head at that moment and Kitty saw his eyes widen and a look of shock registered on his face.

'What the bloody hell's going on here?' he snarled, moving towards them.

He carried a gun and all Kitty could think was that he meant to shoot Sammy with it. She sprang in front of Sammy and held up her hands. Uncle Geoff stopped and didn't come any closer. His expression wavered between bafflement and anger. He lowered the barrel of the gun.

'Get dressed,' he muttered and he turned away as if looking at them disgusted him. Then Kitty saw the gutted rabbit strung across his back, its delicate front feet pointing downwards as if it were diving into the ground.

August 2006

The memory is so vivid and intense that Kitty stops walking. She stands in the street on her way to the postbox and her heart is beating faster than it should. She shakes her head and almost laughs. It seems funny to her now, her mistake, her thinking that Uncle Geoff had hunted them down. *Such bad timing*, she thinks, *Uncle Geoff arriving at that moment. We were so unlucky.* Kitty resumes walking and she thinks about luck and chance and fate and how things might have been different.

June 1944

Kitty had hurriedly put her own shoes on and, even though it did hurt every bit as much as she had expected it to, it no longer mattered. Sammy approached Uncle Geoff in his bare feet and began many sentences of explanation that the older man dismissed with a wave of the gun. He interrupted him with growled reproaches and refused to let him finish.

'Sir, it is not . . . Kitty's feet, sir, she – we got caught in a raid and – look, if you'd just let me —'

The two men circled each other in the moonlight. At last Uncle Geoff yanked his shoulder away from

Sammy's reach and seeing that Kitty had her shoes back on he marched over to her, grabbed hold of her wrist and set off with her down the hill. Sammy called to them to wait for him but, when Uncle Geoff ordered him to clear off, he called, 'Goodnight, Kitty!'

Kitty called back to him, then twisted her arm free and slowed her pace from a trot to a walk. Uncle Geoff stopped and glared at her. 'What in God's name are you thinking of, Kitty? We expected you home hours ago.'

'Sammy was trying to tell you what happened but you wouldn't let him.'

'Now, Kitty, please don't take that tone with me. You have no idea of the danger you were in there.'

Kitty stopped walking. She had been shocked and upset. She had felt something confusingly like guilt, though she knew they had done nothing wrong, but now she felt angry. A storm of rage rose through her body and she turned on her uncle.

'How dare you! I don't even want to think about what you might mean by that. You have no idea – no idea at all. Sammy loves me and I love him, and the only danger I was in was when you came along and waved that gun at us. You could have blown our heads off!'

Kitty pushed past him then and quickly reached the gate at the bottom of the field, which she climbed easily. She was still seething with anger when she reached the house. As she went though the gate, the door opened and Aunt Vi looked out from the dark hallway.

'Oh my dearest girl, there you are, thank goodness. Get inside and let me look at you.'

Aunt Vi led Kitty by the hand down the passageway to the back of the house. In the kitchen she took a long look at Kitty in the gaslight, then hugged her close.

'Oh Aunt Vi, I'm so sorry. We got caught in a raid and it was ages before the all-clear and by then we had missed the bus. We got a lift part of the way then we had to walk.'

Uncle Geoff came in the back door and tossed the rabbit into the sink.

'Go to bed now, young lady,' he said. He didn't look at Kitty as he spoke but turned to hang his jacket on the back door. Kitty had time to glower at his back before Aunt Vi squeezed her hand and held her gaze for a moment.

'Go on – you run along now and get some sleep.'

Upstairs, Kitty locked herself in the bathroom. She got ready for bed slowly. She undressed and washed herself in tepid water, last of all placing her sore and blistered feet one after the other in the sink and letting water from the cold tap run over them. She dried herself and lifted her nightdress from the hook on the back of the door and slipped it over her head. All the while she could hear Aunt Vi and Uncle Geoff talking in the kitchen. When Kitty opened the bathroom door, she was surprised to see Charlie coming up the stairs towards her in his pyjamas. He took the stairs three at a time, treading lightly on the balls of his feet and supporting his weight on the banister rail. His approach was silent and Kitty thought that it was as if he were flying. Arriving on the landing, Kitty saw that his eyes were wide and excited. He gave Kitty a small notebook.

'It's from Sammy. He'll come round and pick it up tomorrow,' he whispered.

Kitty began to question Charlie but at that

moment the kitchen door opened downstairs. Charlie nodded towards Kitty's room and mouthed 'Look outside', before sliding into his bedroom and quietly closing the door.

Kitty went to her window, opened it and leaned out. Sammy was standing in the lane beside the rowan tree. She could see his head and shoulders above the hedge. She waved and he blew her a kiss. Kitty watched Sammy walk away out of sight before closing the window and securing the blackout. She found the matches and lit the candle beside her bed.

Kitty sat down and looked at the book. It was Sammy's logbook and it fell open where a slim pencil was tucked inside. A folded note was there too, a quartered page torn from the back of the book. Kitty saw her name and experienced a rush of joy as she carefully unfolded it. She trailed her finger across the neatly sloping handwriting as she read.

Dearest darling Kitty,

I hope you're okay. Thank you for the best day of my life. I'll see you tomorrow. I love you.

I'm going to need your address – I could find my

way here blindfolded but the postman might need a
bit of help! Write it for me at the back of this book.

Sleep tight,
Sammy x

Kitty read it twice more then tucked it under her pillow. She picked up the pencil, turned to the end of the book and carefully wrote her name and address.

August 2006

Kitty reaches the postbox and, as her letter falls with a soft patter, she wonders if this will be the end of it. It has been unsettling, and she thinks of Bert and recalls what June had said when she phoned to make sure that he was all right.

No point dredging up the past – you can't change anything.

Kitty turns for home. She walks slowly, her arms behind her back, one hand loosely clasping her other arm just above her wrist. She has no plans for the rest of the day and she feels at a loss. There are various jobs to do around the house but she dismisses each one as soon as it comes to mind. She remembers waiting for Sammy to come for the logbook. Her current mood matches the way she felt that morning and she is irresistibly drawn to reliving the memory. Kitty arrives home and decides to go shopping. *Perhaps,* she thinks, *perhaps I can distract myself.*

June 1944

In the morning Uncle Geoff left the house for a trip to Ashford. Some time after he had gone, Kitty looked out of her bedroom window and saw Sammy in the lane. She scuttled down to meet him, rushing through the door as he came in the gate. He grinned when he saw her, and Kitty knew that he was as pleased to see her as she was to see him. They kissed and Sammy lifted her off her feet when he hugged her.

'Are you okay, Kitty? Is your uncle still angry?'

'He has nothing to be angry about – he should have been thanking you for taking care of me.'

Sammy nodded, but said, 'He was taking care of you too, Kitty – in his way. Is he here? I want to talk to him, to explain about last night.'

'You've just missed him, but come and speak to Auntie Vi.'

They went inside and Kitty called out to her aunt as they walked through to the kitchen.

'Is that Sammy I hear with you?'

Aunt Vi was butchering the rabbit and she glanced up at them as they came through the door. Sammy approached the table where Aunt Vi stood with a meat cleaver in her hand. The carcass of the partially jointed animal lay on a wooden block in front of her.

'Mrs Bellamy, I want to apologise for Kitty being so late home last night.'

'Kitty's told me all about it. Sit down, lad. I've got the kettle on the stove. Kitty, make the tea please, dear.'

Kitty took the tin tea caddy from the shelf and set about warming the teapot. *Everything's going to be all right,* she thought. Kitty looked over her shoulder and smiled at the two of them. As she lifted the second spoonful of tea into the pot, Aunt Vi asked Sammy if he knew yet where the war was taking him next. Kitty jumped and caught the spoon on the edge of the caddy. Tea leaves showered across the table.

'Do be careful, Kitty, you know it's like gold dust.' Aunt Vi reached out to a ceramic pot containing wooden spoons and utensils and passed her niece a pastry brush. 'See what you can salvage with that.'

Kitty could sense Sammy watching her as she waited for him to answer Aunt Vi's question. She brushed the scattered leaves into the palm of her hand and transferred them to the teapot. She picked up a cloth and lifted the kettle from the stove. Carefully, she poured the boiling water on to the tea. She did not look up.

'Mrs Bellamy, would you mind if Kitty and I stepped out for a little while? I do have news but, with your permission, I'd like to speak to Kitty about it first – if I may, ma'am?'

Aunt Vi nodded. 'We'll have this tea now it's made and then you can be off. But don't go far – no missed buses today, please.'

Kitty sat opposite Sammy and sipped her tea, swallowing it down past the lump in her throat. At the end of the table Aunt Vi seasoned a saucer of flour and placed the pieces of rabbit in it. She turned each piece over and around until the flesh turned a dusty grey, then she placed it in a skillet.

Sammy's eyes sought out Kitty's but, as soon as her eyes met his and she saw the tenderness there, she looked away. She could feel the need to cry swelling in her chest and behind her eyes.

'Would rabbit be something you have over where you come from, Sammy?' Aunt Vi asked. She placed the skillet on the stove and began peeling and slicing an onion.

'Well, sure, but we usually eat beef and pork. We have a farm, the cows are mostly dairy but we keep some for meat, and there's always a couple of hogs being raised. We've not suffered from short supply like you have in Britain, ma'am.'

Sammy and Aunt Vi continued their conversation while Kitty struggled with her tea. At last Aunt Vi told them to run along. Kitty left the kitchen and headed for the front door where she paused to glance back at Sammy.

'Wait – I'll just fetch your logbook.' She left him abruptly and ran up the stairs. Inside her bedroom, Kitty covered her face with her hands and pressed her fingers against her eyes. She held her breath and willed the tears not to come. She couldn't bear it – it was too hard. They had only just started out – this was their beginning and she could not stand to be separated from Sammy now. Kitty looked in the mirror and dabbed a handkerchief to her eyes. She took a couple of deep breaths and put on some lipstick. She picked up the logbook and went down to meet him.

Sammy had gone outside and, as she came through the front door, he moved to take her in his arms. Kitty let herself be hugged and pulled her mouth into a smile.

'Can we walk a little, please?' she said, handing him the logbook before moving away and heading for the gate. Sammy followed her and they walked in silence. He took her hand and she moved closer and leaned her head towards his shoulder. They walked steadily on, up the hill and out of the village. They continued to walk without speaking and being quiet together made Kitty feel better. When they reached the top gate to the field Kitty stopped. 'Shall we have a look in daylight?'

They climbed into the field and walked around the open barn. They sat down together on the hay bale.

Sammy leaned in and kissed her, then sat up straight again. They looked down the slope of the hill to where some cows cropped the grass. The animals lifted their big heads and stared at them while they chewed then lowered their broad noses to the ground once more. Sammy spoke first.

'You're very brave.'

'I'm trying to be.'

'We're gonna be okay, Kitty – we will be together.'

'Yes.'

He kissed her again.

'A lot of people have it worse than we do.'

'I know.'

'I'll write to you every day – twice a day. Did you write your address for me?'

'Yes, and I'll write back – you'll let me know where to write to, won't you?'

'You bet.'

Sammy put his arm around her shoulders and they sat quietly staring down the field. Crows took off from the copse and flew away out of sight.

'So, when do you have to go?' Kitty asked because suddenly it was impossible not to know.

'Today . . . please don't cry. I was gonna tell you

yesterday, honest I was, but I never found the right
time . . .'

Kitty turned her face to him and though her eyes
were sparkling with tears, she managed to smile.

'I won't cry. I promise – I'm not going to waste
time crying.'

Sammy tucked his hand inside his jacket.

'I've got you something.'

He placed a packet in Kitty's lap and she carefully
unfolded the brown paper.

'Oh, stockings!'

'I don't know if they're the right size or anything
– one of the other guys had some, so . . .'

'They're wonderful, really wonderful. I've never
had stockings before.'

Kitty lifted her face to his and kissed him. Sammy
didn't kiss her back; he closed his eyes and let himself
be kissed. Kitty stayed close to him and studied his
face.

He opened his eyes and grinned. 'I was storing it
up for later – I'm going to remember that kiss. If I'm
ever feeling down, I'll shut my eyes and conjure up
one of your kisses. And I'm going to look for the
moon every night and say goodnight to you.'

'It felt like our moon last night.'

'It was our moon, Kitty – it'll always be our moon. We can look at the moon and it'll be like we are together.'

'Yes.'

Sammy turned towards her and held her hand. 'This is how I see it, Kitty. We'll win this war and we'll win it soon – the news from France is promising. I'll think about you every second and I'll write to you every day.' He stopped to kiss her, then continued. 'And, when it's over, I'll come back and we'll get married. And then some day very soon we'll be in Pennsylvania together and we'll stay at the cabin for our honeymoon. Hell, we'll stay at the cabin for a whole summer – what do you say, Kit? We deserve a summer at least, don't we?'

'Yes,' she said, and there were tears now but she was laughing. 'Yes, Sammy we deserve it, we absolutely deserve it!'

They stayed at the barn making plans until the sun was high in the sky and it was time for Sammy to leave.

'I'll walk you home.'

'No, let's say goodbye here. This is our special place now.'

'Okay, but I'll stay and watch you walk down the hill.'

Kitty agreed and, after starting out then returning to his arms twice, she left him and walked slowly down the field, looking back every few yards to wave at him and blow him a kiss. Sammy climbed a stack of bales behind their seat and waved at her.

'See you soon,' he yelled. 'I love you.'

August 2006

Kitty sets out on her shopping trip. It is hot and airless in the car and she opens both windows as soon as she has started the engine. She lifts a lever beneath the steering wheel and soapy water sprays the dirty glass. The wipers leap from side to side and two glistening and transparent arcs appear in the dusty windscreen. She is soon driving past apple orchards where the fruit has ripened early and the trees droop in weary rows. She joins a slip lane, indicates and pulls on to the dual carriageway and heads for Maidstone.

June 1944

Kitty arrived home to find Dora sitting on the gate. She jumped down and ran to meet Kitty, slipping her arm through Kitty's and leading her away from the house.

'Oh Kitty – the most awful thing's happened. My mother is with your Aunt Vi getting advice because she doesn't know what to do for the best, and father is inconsolable. Mother says that your aunt is a sensible person and a good sort and that she won't gossip. I'm not supposed to know anything about it, but I heard them talking last night. You won't believe it when I tell you.'

Dora paused then as she noticed the packet of nylon stockings in Kitty's hand.

'That's where you've been – walking out with your pilot!' She looked around her in case Sammy was nearby. Dora took the stockings from Kitty and turned the packet over in her hand.

'What's happened, Dora? Tell me, for goodness' sake.'

Dora passed the stockings back to Kitty and leaned forwards so that her mouth was close to Kitty's ear.

'It's Gwen,' she whispered, 'she's going to have a baby.'

August 2006

The turning to the town centre passes by on the left and Kitty drives on. At the next junction she glances at the sign to the multi-storey car park but chooses to ignore it. This is not a shopping trip despite what she had told herself when she set off. Ten minutes later, she parks outside June's house and sits for a moment, one hand rests on the handbrake, the other hovers near the key which she has left in the ignition. She thinks through what she will say to June. *Just passing, thought I'd pop in.* She worries what June will say to this, for June specifically asked her not to come.

As soon as she gets out of her car, she hears the thud and boom of loud music. She tries the doorbell and is not surprised when no one comes. No one can hear her. She presses the doorbell again, longer this time, and almost immediately the door opens. A young man stares down at her. He looks as if he has just woken up. His hair sticks up, uncombed, and he wears tracksuit bottoms and no shirt. He greets Kitty with a raised lip and screwed up nose – a comedy expression of enquiry unaccompanied by words.

Kitty tries to speak, but the music blasts through the open doorway and she has no idea whether she makes a sound or merely opens her mouth. The youth turns and pads off on bare feet. Kitty sees the smoothness of his back and the grey Calvin Klein waistband of his underwear. Suddenly it is silent and he returns to the door.

'Mum's out shopping.' His eyes flit across Kitty's face and rest on something at some distance behind her.

'I'm sorry to disturb you. Martin, is it?' Kitty smiles and the young man shuffles from foot to foot and waits for more from her.

'I'm a friend of your grandad. I was wondering how he is?'

Martin frowns, his gaze falls to the ground somewhere near Kitty's feet.

'I don't know – he's all right.' He nods and sways as if he still hears the music. He makes a move to close the door and Kitty puts out her hand.

'I was going to ask your mother if she thought I might visit him after all – I'll be careful not to tire him. I would just like to see for myself how he is.'

Martin shuffles round and dips his hand into a china dish on a shelf behind him and pulls out a key.

'All right?' he asks as he holds the key out and reaches to close the door with his other hand. Kitty hesitates, then takes the key and turns to go; the music resumes as she passes through the gate and she thinks that she can still hear the faint boom of it when she reaches Bert's home. She lets herself in with the key.

'Hello? Bert, it's Kitty.'

'Oh Kitty!' His reply is earnest. 'Oh, thank goodness, Kitty,' he says as she appears in the doorway of his sunroom. Bert reaches for his stick, balances it against his knee and starts to stand. He presses his large hands into the arms of his chair and his shoulders begin to tremble as he rises. Kitty hurries towards him.

'Please don't get up, Bert. Are you all right? June told me that you weren't at all well after my last visit.'

'I'm all right. I'm all right – it's you, Kitty. I've been so worried about you.'

Bert sinks back into the chair and blinks away tears.

'Whatever for, Bert? You don't want to worry about me. I'm fine.'

'I am so sorry, Kitty. Sit down . . . I have to tell you something.'

'Yes, all right, but please don't upset yourself – there's to be no more talk about the war. June rang me to say that she thought I'd better not come at all, because it had upset you so much last time. And I nearly didn't come except I wanted to see how you are and I thought I could cheer you up.'

Bert's eyes narrow in anger. He takes several noisy gasps of air through his open mouth before he speaks.

'She had no right – June shouldn't have – we have

to talk about it – it's been covered up for too long. Too long.' Bert coughs and reaches for a handkerchief and, as he wipes his eyes and the spittle from his chin, Kitty wonders what he has to tell her and suddenly feels afraid to hear it.

'It was after the flying bomb, you see, Kitty – what it did to your brother and that, it was meant to be for the best – that's what he thought – at the time that's what we all thought.'

Kitty sits perched on the edge of her seat but, as she begins to consider the meaning of what Bert is telling her, she slides back into the chair and reaches for the armrests because she feels as though she is falling.

June 1944

Uncle Geoff picked up the knife, stabbed a slice of bread and held it out across the table at Kitty.

'Late home for his tea last night and not here for breakfast . . .'

Kitty took the bread and Uncle Geoff made a quick bayonet-jab into the next slice and held it up in Aunt Vi's direction. 'Did you hear him go out this morning, Vi? If he's not back before I'm ready to leave, he'll spend the day digging ditches with an empty belly and it'll serve him right.'

Since D-Day Charlie had hardly been at home. On the afternoon that the invasion began, he cycled miles exploring the deserted staging camps, fascinated by the evidence of rapid departure. There were guards at the field gates but, leaving his bicycle and crossing through the trees behind one camp, Charlie was able to wander through empty Nissen huts that a day ago had been full of men.

In one he discovered a piece of wood, the size of a cricket ball that had been half-carved into a bear – unfinished and left behind. The carver had seen the potential in the wood, a curve in a branch like a swollen elbow suggesting the haunches of the animal. The head and back were complete, but the underside and legs were roughly hewn as if the bear had yet to come fully to life and walk free of its mould. Charlie brought it home and that night began whittling wood with his pocket knife. He sat by the fire in the evenings, skinning the bark from sticks and flicking the curls into the flames.

The front door opened then banged shut and Charlie appeared in the doorway of the small dining room beside the kitchen. He was flushed and glistening with sweat. His short-cropped dark hair was shrouded in dust and smudges of grime marked his face.

'They're waterproofing the tanks up the road at Broughton's!' He grinned at them, then his gaze fell immediately to the table. 'I'm starving.'

'Have you forgotten that you're working for Tom Farrell today?' Uncle Geoff asked. 'I'm leaving in one minute.'

'Go and wash before you think of sitting at the table,' said Aunt Vi as she set about pouring Charlie a cup of tea.

They heard the jet of water from the kitchen tap blasting into the stone sink and Charlie shouted to them over the noise of it.

'One of the soldiers, Solly – he's my friend, he told me that they're going over soon, any day now. They've had orders to stand to.'

Returning to the room, he flung himself into his chair at the table. Immediately reaching for his teacup, he raised it to his lips while simultaneously reaching for a slice of bread with his other hand.

'They're a mobile workshop. As we push the Nazis out of France, they'll follow the front line, fixing up the damaged tanks.' Charlie spread a spoonful of jam on his bread and took another slice, which he pressed on top of it.

'I'm to go back later.' He took a large mouthful and gobbled it down, turning to Aunt Vi. 'Solly said I should take some more cherries – the orchard's full of them and they've been told to pick what they can before they go.'

Uncle Geoff stood up. 'Come on, lad, let's get on now. I told Tom we'd be there at eight.'

Charlie downed his tea and followed his uncle, taking his bread and jam with him.

'We'll have a job to make more jam, Kitty,' remarked Aunt Vi. 'We're all but out of sugar. I'll see if your uncle can get a couple of rabbits so as we can make a swap. The next thing you know, the raspberries will be ripening.'

Charlie had taken to visiting the soldiers who were camped in the orchards at Broughton Farm whenever he could, and had brought home cherries by the pound which Auntie Vi and Kitty had made into pies and jam. As Kitty ate the cherries, she kept a tally with the rhyme – *Tinker, tailor, soldier, sailor, rich man, poor man, beggarman, thief* – smiling to herself when she ate the third and imagining herself married to Sammy. If she ate on, she kept account of the rhyme in her head – happy to pause at *rich man* but always eating on until she could stop at *soldier*.

She hadn't seen Sammy since the day after they went together to Ashford when he had come to say goodbye. But, as he had promised, a letter arrived for her each morning and some days she received two. His letters began, *Kitty, my darling* or, *My dearest, darling Kitty* and ended, *All my love, ever yours, Sammy* – and those words popped into her head at any given moment each day, filling her with a happiness that made her giddy.

One morning, a week or so after D-Day, as Aunt Vi stirred the preserving pan over the heat and the sickly-sweet smell of cherries and sugar filled the air, they heard the chugging drone of passing aircraft. Kitty had been cutting circles of greaseproof paper and she dropped the scissors and ran outside. Directly overhead was a dark plane trailing a red flame. It passed over the house and was followed by another. A fighter plane appeared and tailed the second. Kitty watched until they were out of sight. She was shielding her eyes with her hand and staring into the sky when Aunt Vi came to the door.

'What was it? Did you see?' she asked.

'I don't know . . .' Kitty struggled to describe it. 'It was strange, two planes with flames out the back.'

'What do you mean – were they on fire?'

'No, I don't think so.'

'Well,' said Auntie Vi, 'they certainly sounded strange – more like enormous motorbikes.'

They returned to the kitchen and Kitty was bothered by what she had seen and the uncomfortable feeling stayed with her all day.

That night, before she went to sleep she read Sammy's letters. She read each of them through in order and, when she got to the last one, she went back to the first and read them all again. She read on until her eyes were closing and then she slipped the bundle of letters beneath her pillow as she fell asleep.

Kitty had been dreaming, a dream where Sammy had been with her and they were happy. It was not a dream she would recall. The explosion ripped her from sleep to wakefulness, so that she stood fully alert and shaking beside her bed, her bare feet staggering on the linoleum. She had no idea what had happened to her. Coming to her senses, she heard Charlie's bedroom door wrenched open and banged shut. Uncle Geoff and Aunt Vi's voices called from their bedroom as she hurried on to the landing. Charlie hurtled downstairs, pulling on his clothes before yanking open the front door.

'Charlie, Charlie, wait!' Kitty called as she rushed to the bottom of the stairs. 'Do you think that was a plane coming down?'

'Stay here, Kit. I'll go and find out.'

Charlie disappeared into the dawn and Kitty ran to get dressed. Her heart leaped painfully behind her ribs and her hands shook as she struggled to fasten buttons. All the while, one sentence repeated itself over and over in her head. *Please, please not Sammy. Please, please not Sammy. Please, please not Sammy . . .*

It was a beautiful morning and the sky was a brilliant clear blue, but up ahead a black and billowing pall of smoke climbed vertically into the air. As Kitty ran down the road, she heard two smaller explosions – the first made her stop dead in her tracks, then the second, following the first by half a minute, had her running again as fast as she could go.

She took the uphill curve in the road, panting hard, and passed the spot where she had fallen from

Charlie's bicycle. It had been a matter of weeks ago, she still had red scars on her knees, but Kitty felt utterly disconnected from the girl cycling home from choir. She could hear shouts up ahead now and she turned one more bend and found herself at the gated entrance to Broughton's Farm and her eye fell on two things. The first, she recognised immediately – Charlie's bicycle thrown against the hedge. The second object mystified her.

She was breathing hard and gradually recovering her breath while staring at the peculiarly displaced object that hung above her head in the tree beside the gate post. It was a pale and creamy cylinder, the size of an umbrella stand and encircled at both ends by what seemed to be a withered garland of red and blue roses. She puzzled over it for several seconds until, suddenly, it came to her what it was. It was someone's leg. Kitty let out a small cry and turned her head away and looked now through the open gates into the chaos of the camp.

Everywhere there were men, some were running – some staggered around with blood on their faces or pouring down their arms. Others sat with their heads in their hands and still more lay groaning on the grass. Some, she could tell by the twisted distortion of their bodies, and heads pressed face down into the ground, were dead. Then, an officer came hurrying towards her with his arms outstretched, as if she were a goose he wished to shoo into a pen.

'This is no place for you, go home.'

Kitty pulled herself together, stood up straight and looked him in the eye. 'I can help – I can dress wounds.'

Aunt Vi and Uncle Geoff arrived then. Aunt Vi climbed out of the car carrying a bundle of sheets, blankets and towels and the officer pointed towards the farmhouse.

'I've been directing men with minor injuries over there – Mrs Markham will be pleased of your help. I'll send a medic over shortly.' Then he spoke to Uncle Geoff. 'Sir, I'm Captain Horton. I'm going to have to requisition your vehicle to help transport the walking wounded to the cottage hospital at Canterbury.'

Kitty took half of what Aunt Vi carried and hurried with her across the orchard towards the farmhouse. Glancing back over her shoulder, she surveyed the scene behind her. Nissen huts had been flung aside in the blast or had collapsed where they stood, as if made from matchsticks and trodden underfoot. Entangled in the debris were electricity cables, their severed ends burning with a brilliant blue flame.

The impact had come at reveille and men had been going about their morning activities. One young man, wearing a greatcoat over his underwear, was searching among the ruins of a destroyed washroom. He repeatedly bent down as if to pick something up, then stood again empty-handed, saying, 'I can't find my shoes. Has anyone seen my shoes?'

Kitty looked for Charlie among the confusion but couldn't see him.

The evenings that Kitty had spent at the church hall learning first aid were poor preparation for the task before her and it was Aunt Vi who made the better nurse. Mrs Markham bustled to and from her kitchen bringing the things that Aunt Vi needed to bathe cuts and pull splinters of wood, and shards of glass and metal. And all the while Kitty spoke to the men, asking them about their homes and families, telling them about her life in Kent, her home in London, the jars of cherry jam they were making. There was something beguiling about Kitty when she spoke. The gentle, musical rise and fall of her voice seemed to soothe the men and they were calm and sipped the hot sweet tea that Mrs Markham brought them.

Captain Horton came to them after a few hours and thanked them. 'Will you kindly follow me, ladies. I wish to speak to you before you go.'

Kitty and Aunt Vi followed him into the kitchen. Uncle Geoff was sitting at the table cradling a mug of tea in his gnarled hands. Mrs Markham pulled out chairs for Aunt Vi and Kitty and placed cups of tea in front of them. Two elderly men stood in a corner, holding their hats in their hands, their eyes lowered.

'Where's Charlie?' Kitty asked.

'Charlie?'

'Her brother, our nephew,' replied Aunt Vi. 'He arrived here before us this morning.'

'Ah yes, he helped as a stretcher bearer – I'll have someone find him.' The Captain cleared his throat before continuing. 'I am asking that you do not discuss any details of the tragedy that you have witnessed here this morning with other persons – neither military personnel nor civilians. We are very grateful for your help and I shall be including you all in my report, but it is of the utmost importance that no information about what has occurred here becomes available to enemy intelligence. So, I have to ask that you go about your daily business as if none of this happened. Is that understood by everyone?'

They nodded and murmured their assent and Captain Horton excused himself.

Uncle Geoff and Kitty waited quietly, finishing their tea, while Aunt Vi talked to Mrs Markham. Then the three of them walked slowly to the gate and waited beside it for Charlie.

'I've not had time to think about Charlie,' said Aunt Vi and she began to tut and sigh.

Uncle Geoff patted her shoulder and said, 'Now then, he'll be all right.'

Without thinking, Kitty glanced up into the tree but the gruesome object had gone, and she half wondered if she had imagined it. She folded her arms around herself and turned to look again into the camp. She watched a guardsman sorting through wreckage and slinging planks of wood into different piles. A thin soldier swept the cleared concrete base of a Nissen hut with a broom, stopping every few sweeps to run his hand across his eyes. Near him another man was welding.

The shouts of a group of men drew Kitty's attention. They had roped a tipped-over truck and were yelling to each other about the best way to right it. Beyond them, a mess table had been set up and cooking smells were beginning to waft across the orchard, carried on the gentle morning breeze. Kitty saw Captain Horton talking to a young soldier. The Captain glanced over and met her gaze and then dismissed the soldier. Kitty watched him walking towards them.

'Apparently your lad's not been seen for a while – I'm sorry, what with the confusion and everything, but Corporal Harman thinks he went home over an hour ago.'

'He's only fifteen,' Aunt Vi said quietly.

Kitty walked through the gate then and out on to the road.

'Uncle Geoff!' she called. 'Charlie's bicycle – it's still here.'

August 2006

Bert has not been able to look at Kitty while she speaks. He listens as she recounts what she saw and stares down into his lap. Then he tells her what he knows and has always known about the day that the bomb fell on Broughton Farm.

'The V1 was shot down, Kitty.'

Kitty removes her glasses; her hands are trembling. She blinks away her tears and reaches into her handbag for a tissue.

'Yes, I heard that rumoured, I think that's what Uncle Geoff thought had happened.'

Bert lifts his head and watches her and his blue

eyes are troubled and enquiring.

'It was shot down by an American – it was Sammy, Kit. Sammy shot down the flying bomb.'

Kitty gasps and stares at him. Bert's head wavers as if it is suddenly too heavy for his neck. He leans forward, his elbows stick out, his hands grasp the arm wings and he begins the slow, painful process of standing.

'I'm sorry, Kitty. I thought that you must have known and that you had agreed not to see Sammy anymore. But when you said the other day about him having a sweetheart back home and that you thought that he didn't really care for you – saying about him coming to his senses and going back to her – I realised then that you didn't know anything. I saw how terrible it must have been for you to think that he'd just disappeared without a word. But it wasn't like that at all. He didn't forget you, Kitty.'

Bert has risen from his chair and, taking up his stick, he shuffles to the door. Kitty sits as if dazed.

'Can I make you some tea, Kitty?'

Slowly, Kitty follows him to the kitchen where Bert opens a drawer and takes something from it. It is Kitty who moves to the sink and fills the kettle.

'I, I knew about it, later on – that the fighter planes brought down the V1s. But no one told me at the time that Sammy . . . that . . . that Sammy . . .' She begins to cry again.

'Well, it wasn't common knowledge obviously, everything was hushed up.'

Bert gradually, shakily, lowers himself into a chair at the kitchen table. Kitty pulls out a chair and sits opposite him. She blows her nose and sits straighter.

'Tell me, Bert, please tell me everything – I want to know everything now. Was . . . was Sammy hurt?'

'No, no, he wasn't. He was lucky there. Many pilots died shooting down V1 rockets; they got caught in the blast. In those first few weeks after D-Day any pilot would have a go at them – later on, when we knew more about them, the RAF put Hawker Tempests on to them.'

'Yes,' Kitty interrupts him, 'but what about Sammy? What happened to Sammy?'

'Well, he'd been coming back in from an escort mission when he spotted it over the Channel and his team leader sent him after it. His brief was to stop it getting to London at all costs. He was a pilot in war-time doing his duty – but he knew he was close to

163

your house, he tried to bring it down over open land.'

'Would he have known how many men died at Broughton? Poor Sammy. I don't know how he could have lived with that.'

'He knew and he knew about Charlie too . . .'

Bert tries to say something else but his voice falters. He tries again and begins to cough. Kitty stands and gets him a glass of water from the kitchen tap. She returns to the table and sees an envelope in Bert's hands.

'I'm afraid that you might not be able to forgive me, Kitty. I hope you can – but I'll not blame you if you can't. I think what we did was wrong now, but at the time, with you so young and all – we thought it was best for you.'

'What are you trying to say, Bert? And who is *we*? Whom are you talking about?' She places the glass of water on the table beside Bert and sits.

'Me and your Uncle Geoff – it was wrong. What we did was wrong.'

'Uncle Geoff?' Kitty feels her heart begin to beat harder. 'What's Uncle Geoff got to do with anything?'

'Sammy gave me a letter for you, Kitty, but your

Uncle Geoff wouldn't give it to you. He said that Sammy would ruin your life and it was best if you didn't hear from him anymore. Best to do it then before you got any more involved. He said that you were young and you'd get over it. I tried to reason with him, but he said thousands of girls were being let down and worse by Yank boyfriends and we'd be doing you a favour.'

Kitty slowly shakes her head as she remembers Gwendolyn and the son she raised alone in England, not in Chicago as her GI boyfriend had promised. But Bert is still speaking and she turns her attention back to what he is telling her.

'Geoff said that you weren't strong and it would be burdening you with nothing but sorrow and, God knows, Kitty, I saw enough of those young pilots die – they left girlfriends, fiancées, wives – he wanted to protect you from that. Geoff refused to take Sammy's letter from me. He said you weren't to have it. He told me to destroy it. I am so sorry, Kitty. I thought he knew what was best for you.'

Kitty stares at Bert and then at the manila envelope that he holds towards her. It waves in his trembling hand and Kitty sits and frowns at it. She does not understand and, seeing her confusion, Bert says, 'It's for you . . . from Sammy . . . it's the letter, Kitty, the one he wrote to you. I couldn't destroy it – it didn't seem right to do that.'

Kitty gasps and one hand flies to her mouth, but the other reaches out to Bert and takes hold of the letter. She pulls it to her lap and sees the familiar handwriting before it blurs.

June 1944

The search for Charlie continued through the day and into the night. Uncle Geoff and Tom Farrell drove round the lanes and out to the nearest villages checking the barns and outhouses. They came home for meals and looked in whenever they passed by in case he had come home. Meanwhile, Aunt Vi and Kitty stayed at the house and waited in case Charlie returned. As the day wore on into afternoon and then evening, Aunt Vi became increasingly distressed. She seemed to have lost her capacity to cope, and it was Kitty who spoke reassuringly, made them all dinner and later, tea, while Aunt Vi paced the rooms, stopping suddenly when she thought of somewhere Charlie might be, or when she was convinced that she had heard him outside.

'Do you think that we should have left the bicycle where it was?' Aunt Vi studied Kitty's face for an answer.

'It's not far to walk – he'll guess that we brought it back,' Kitty replied.

'But you know how he is about that machine. I don't understand why he would leave it.'

'Please don't fret, Auntie. Shall I make us some more tea?'

Gradually, anxiously, the long day passed until finally, well after ten o'clock at night, Tom Farrell dropped Uncle Geoff back at the house.

'I think we should call London and get a message to your mother, Kitty,' Aunt Vi said when the clock struck eleven.

Uncle Geoff disagreed. 'You'll give her the scare of her life. And what can she do from there? Nothing. Anyhow, knowing that boy, he'll like as not turn up by morning, happy as Larry.'

'And what if he doesn't turn up? What do I say to Win? Oh, we lost him yesterday, but we thought we wouldn't worry you with it until Geoff decided that he wasn't coming back!' And, as she said this, Aunt Vi snatched a cup from the dresser and moved it to a different hook. In a moment she had snatched up another and soon all the cups were swinging on their hooks. Neither her niece nor her husband could understand her intention as Aunt Vi continued to swap the cups around until each hung in a new place.

'I think that perhaps we should telephone Mum in the morning,' Kitty said gently.

'Yes, that's right, Kit, that's what we'll do,' said Aunt Vi, frowning at the dresser, not yet happy with how it looked.

Uncle Geoff and Aunt Vi went to bed and Kitty lay awake in the next room, listening to the murmur of their voices through the wall – Uncle Geoff's low and constant, Aunt Vi's by turns shrill and urgent then muffled, despairing.

Kitty could not sleep. When she closed her eyes she saw the leg in the tree. She pulled out Sammy's letters from beneath her pillow but she didn't read them. It didn't feel right to her to wander into that state of mind where only she and Sammy existed and nothing else mattered. But the thought of Sammy made her realise that she could not lie in bed and wait for morning while Charlie was missing. And, thinking what Sammy would do, she got up and dressed quietly in the dark. Holding her breath and avoiding the creaky stair, Kitty went down and let herself out to look for her brother.

Kitty wheeled Charlie's bicycle away from the house before climbing on to it and pedalling towards the village. Aunt Vi was right – it was odd that he had left the bicycle behind. Kitty couldn't understand why he would do that either. As she pedalled, she thought about Charlie and tried to imagine being him. What would he do? Where would he go? She tried not to think about what he would have seen at Broughton that morning, but she knew that that would be part of it. Charlie had known those men – he had been proud to know them. The wheels crunched on the gritty road and Kitty gripped the handlebars and pushed on the pedals and thought about how it would feel to be Charlie.

When, at last, it came to her, it seemed so obvious she couldn't believe that it had taken her so long to think of it. Charlie was on his way to France – he hadn't taken his bicycle because he wasn't planning on coming back.

Just as she had this revelation, Kitty saw a faint light flickering in the church graveyard. She slowed to a halt and dismounted the bicycle and left it leaning against the wall beside the lych-gate. Instinctively, she avoided the gravel pathway and stepped silently across the grass towards the dusky figures moving purposefully in the lantern-lit scene ahead of her. She recognised the tall, lean form of Captain Horton. He was writing on a clipboard while beside him a guardsman held up a lantern.

The glow lit the officer's face and Kitty saw a man who was just managing to control his emotion. His forehead was furrowed with lines and his lips were rolled inward and pressed together. He stood on the edge of an enormous grave, several metres square and deep, so that only the heads and shoulders of the gravediggers were visible near Captain Horton's feet.

Kitty watched as two soldiers approached carrying a stretcher. They lowered a shrouded body into the arms of the soldiers in the grave. Behind them more soldiers approached. Kitty watched on as, one after another, bodies were lowered into the earth. It was so quiet that she could hear the laboured breathing of the burial party and the Captain's pencil scratch across the paper as he recorded the names of the men he would now be leaving in England.

Kitty began to cry and bit against her knuckle to keep quiet. She tried to count the bodies as they were passed downwards but became lost as more than fifty men were lowered into the dark earth. At last the guardsmen climbed out of the ground and a weary assembly pulled themselves to attention beside the mass grave. Captain Horton read a committal prayer.

It occurred to Kitty that it was dreadful that she was the only ordinary person to witness this secret ceremony. She began to imagine the grief of the countless women and girls involved in the lives of these dead men. How many sisters, mothers, daughters, sweethearts and wives would soon be hearing that their loved one had been killed? And the thought that these women did not yet know, that tomorrow they would wake hopeful and ignorant of their loss, began to overwhelm Kitty. She felt a wave of unbearable sadness surge through her; a physical pain as if her ribcage might suddenly split open and she could not bear it. It was as if she alone bore the burden of grief for three generations of women. And with the grief came a terrifying dread that she too might have cause to mourn and the knowledge that she was powerless to protect the men she loved. The horror of it engulfed her and she cried out and fell to the ground.

Kitty came back to herself as one of the soldiers, hearing her cry, reached her, and the lantern he carried revealed her kneeling and wretched in the damp grass. More men came to her side and someone helped her to her feet.

'I'm so sorry, I'm so sorry,' she said through her sobs.

They hushed her and told her that it would be all right, each man repeating a version of a platitude that he felt little conviction for.

'Come and pray with us – do you feel well enough?' Captain Horton studied her with serious eyes. Kitty nodded and they walked back to the grave. The servicemen stood to attention while the officer led them in the Lord's Prayer and then recited:

'They shall grow not old, as we that are left grow
  old:
Age shall not weary them, nor the years condemn.

At the going down of the sun and in the morning
We will remember them.'

Captain Horton led Kitty away as the men slowly took up the spades and began to fill in the grave.

'I'll get Harman to drive you home. What are you doing wandering around at night anyway?' Before she answered, he called out and the Corporal hurried towards them.

'I couldn't sleep, I was looking for my brother,' Kitty said.

'Good God – has he not turned up yet?'

'No, but I think I know now – I think he will want to go to France – to fight. After the . . . after this morning, Charlie will have wanted to go and do his bit – he has said so before, since D-Day, and before that really.'

'How old is he? Seventeen?'

'No, he's fifteen – he'll not be sixteen till Christmas.'

The Captain told Harman to bring transport to take Kitty and the bicycle home.

'Well, I shouldn't worry too much. If he tries to enlist they'll send him home to you. I can put word out if you like. Warn the local boards to be on the lookout for him.'

Kitty thanked him.

'And remember – you're not to speak of this?'

'Yes, but can I ask you one thing? Charlie spoke of someone called Solly – one of your men. Do you know if he – did he . . . ?'

'I'm afraid the man you're speaking of was killed this morning. I'm sorry.'

Kitty nodded and moved towards the waiting vehicle when she thought of something else.

'And can you tell me . . . when will they know . . . the families of . . . ?'

It was too dark to see his face properly and, when he didn't answer for several seconds, Kitty thought that she had asked too much and should apologise. As she went to speak he gave his reply.

'Soon.'

Kitty asked to be set down at the corner because she did not want to wake her aunt and uncle. Her head was throbbing, and as she wheeled the bicycle through the gate and left it under the lean-to beside the house, she began to shiver. By the time she was in bed, her trembling had become out of control and caused her teeth to chatter. Her head was sticky with perspiration. She felt cold and sick. Kitty pulled the covers over her shoulders and tucked her knees up to her chest. *Had Charlie found Solly's body that morning? What horror had he witnessed?* Again, the image of the severed leg returned. Kitty moaned out loud.

'Oh, where are you, Charlie? Where are you?'

The next morning Kitty could barely lift her head from her pillow.

Thinking that she must be exhausted after the previous day's ordeal, Aunt Vi left her to sleep. Soon after nine o'clock, she came to Kitty's bedroom bringing a letter from Sammy and found her niece lying awake with a fever.

'Dear child, whatever's wrong with you!' cried Aunt Vi, as she opened the curtains and the sunlight fell on Kitty's puffy face. She quickly closed the curtains again and went to Kitty's bedside. She touched the back of her fingers against her niece's forehead and exclaimed at the heat emanating from her. Kitty could not speak above a whisper, her throat was sore and her neck was swollen. She managed to tell Aunt Vi where she thought Charlie had gone.

'Come on, let's get you to the bathroom and into a clean nightdress.'

Kitty whimpered as she moved; every joint and muscle ached and her throat felt as though it had been scrubbed with wire wool. As Aunt Vi helped her from the bed she began to shiver and shake. Aunt Vi held her round the waist and gently coaxed her out to the landing.

'Come on, sweetheart, that's my girl. There now, we'll get you better.'

In the face of Kitty's illness, Aunt Vi recovered her resourcefulness. After helping Kitty to the toilet, she washed her and dressed her in a clean nightdress. She sat Kitty in the chair with a blanket over her while she stripped the sodden sheets from Kitty's bed and remade it with fresh linen. She sent Uncle Geoff to call out the doctor and got busy in the kitchen. Soon, the smell of simmering soup filled the house.

'Now then, Kitty love,' Aunt Vi said as she carried a tray into the room and placed it beside the bed. 'I want you to try and gargle for me – it's just warm salty water. Come on, dear – you've got to, it'll help you get better.'

Kitty allowed herself to be helped up until she

rested on her elbow. She opened her mouth as Aunt Vi raised a cup to her lips and held a bowl beneath her chin. Kitty tried to tip her head back but, as the salt water hit the raw flesh of her throat, the shock of the sting made her gasp and the water poured from her mouth into the bowl. Kitty shuddered and began to cry.

'Now then, sweetheart, come on, crying won't do you any good. It's just going to make you feel worse, that's all.' Aunt Vi took the bowl away and wiped her chin. She raised a spoon to Kitty's lips. 'This is just some warmed honey with an aspirin crushed into it – try and get it down dear, come along.'

Kitty took the honey mixture and sank back on to her pillow. She closed her eyes while Aunt Vi stroked her hair back from her brow. She fell asleep.

Aunt Vi glanced in the hall mirror as she tied her headscarf and repeated her instructions that Uncle Geoff was to keep an eye on Kitty until she got back. 'And what did the doctor say?'

'He'll drop in this afternoon,' Uncle Geoff called from the kitchen as he peered inside the stockpot.

'Out of there,' Aunt Vi said from the hallway as

she recognised the sound of the pan lid being lifted. 'I'm making that for Kitty – there's bread and a bit of luncheon meat for you.' Aunt Vi put her head round the kitchen door. 'I'm worried about that girl, Geoff – I hope it's not diphtheria.'

'Oh, she'll be all right, Vi,' he answered irritably.

'Well, I hope so. I'm going to ask Mrs Parkes if I can borrow her telephone and get a message to Win. To think that last night I was lying awake wondering how on earth I could tell her about Charlie, and now there's Kit too.' She sighed. 'I won't be long.'

It was while Aunt Vi was out using Mrs Parkes' telephone and Kitty slept feverishly upstairs that Sammy came to the house.

August 2006

Bert tells Kitty about Sammy's visit the day after the V1 was shot down. Kitty sits quietly in Bert's kitchen where a wall clock ticks loudly and the tap drips intermittently. She hears how Sammy, after pursuing the flying bomb and shooting it down, returned to his base in East Anglia and learned of the casualties in the debrief. Bert tells Kitty that Sammy risked a court martial when he took a plane and flew to Kent after the next day's operations.

'I felt sorry for the lad, Kitty. I took the letter and said I'd get it to you. But your Uncle Geoff wasn't having any of it. I let him convince me. I didn't see Sammy again after that – his lot were sent to Italy.'

Kitty takes a deep breath and lifts her chin to meet Bert's gaze. She attempts a smile.

'Do you know, Bert . . . in a funny way, it's a relief.' She glances down at the envelope in her hands. 'It never made any sense to me that Sammy could just disappear from my life.' She begins to nod slowly then says softly, 'I was very ill after the tragedy at Broughton – I had a fever. The doctor said it was tonsillitis but that it was compounded by nervous exhaustion. But, when I was well enough, I wrote to Sammy twice a day but I never heard back.' A look of horror crosses Kitty's face. 'Uncle Geoff took my letters to the post office. Do you think he . . . ?'

'Well, I don't know about that,' Bert says, shaking his head. They fall quiet while the ticking clock measures the pause in their conversation. After a minute Bert says, 'You know, Betty and I saw quite a bit of Geoff and Vi, after the war. Geoff and I played darts every Friday at the Queen's Head. Whenever I asked after you, Kitty, it was all good. He was proud of you and said you were doing well.'

Bert leans across the table towards her. 'Do you remember that August Bank Holiday we met you and Vi in Hastings, when your little girl was small? In the early Sixties it would have been. You made such a lovely family – I thought then that it had all been for the best. I had forgotten I even had the letter until last week.' Bert stops speaking and looks hard at Kitty. Then he brings his hands to his face and draws them up his cheeks and over the dome of his head.

'I am sorry, Kitty, I didn't think it was my place – you know, back then, to question what Geoff wanted to do.'

'But, you let me have the book – do you remember that, Bert? After Broughton, after they found Charlie, I begged Aunt Vi to go to the airbase and find out what had happened to Sammy and you gave her the book to give to me.'

'I thought no harm in giving you that – as a memento, like.'

'But you had the letter then?'

Bert moves uncomfortably in his chair and his chin trembles. 'Oh, Kitty I'm sorry. I had promised Geoff, you see – he was fiercely adamant that you weren't to have it. I promised him that I wouldn't give it to you.'

Kitty does not think before she says what comes to her mind. 'And you promised Sammy that you would.'

June 1944

Uncle Geoff looked up from his raspberry canes as Sammy arrived at the gate. He straightened his back, took a quick glance up at Kitty's window, and then went to meet the younger man. Seeing him approach, Sammy stopped at the gate and held out his hand in greeting.

'She's not here,' Uncle Geoff said as he wiped his hands on his thighs and levelled his gaze at Sammy. The boy looked terrible. His eyes had sunk into his face; he was gaunt and pale. There was a look of desperation about him.

'She's not here?' he repeated and peered past Uncle

Geoff towards the house.

'Charlie's gone missing. Seems like he's run off to enlist.'

'Charlie? But, he's too young.' Sammy's eyes flicked from Uncle Geoff to the house and back again.

'Looks old enough though, doesn't he? He might fool anybody, size of that lad.'

'When will Kitty be back?'

'I couldn't say. Now, if you'll excuse me, I've got work to do.'

Uncle Geoff began to turn away, but Sammy reached out and caught hold of his shoulder.

'Please! Please . . . sir, I have to see her. It's real important.'

Uncle Geoff moved towards the gate and leaned his face into Sammy's.

'Just leave the girl alone, can't you? You know you're going to break her heart.'

Sammy's head jerked backward as if he had been hit. He began shaking his head in denial.

'No sir, I've no intention of . . . This isn't what I wanted to say right now, like this, but I mean to marry Kitty, sir. I love her.'

'She's sixteen years old – you've swept her off her feet. You're going to ruin that girl's life and you know it.'

'No, you've got me all wrong. I'd never do anything to hurt Kitty. I want to look after her and make her happy.'

'So you say – but she wasn't being looked after the night you brought her home from Ashford. Lord knows what sort of carry on —'

'No, sir, it wasn't like you say at all, there was never —'

Uncle Geoff raised his hand, pointed his finger in Sammy's face and interrupted him.

'You're thinking about yourself, about what *you* want. You're not thinking about Kitty at all!'

They stood facing each other with the closed gate between them. Uncle Geoff spoke in low clipped tones. 'So you survive the war – are you going to marry Kitty and settle down in England?'

'Well, we've talked about going back home – you see there's the farm and —'

'You've talked? Have you? Have you really? Did she tell you that their father died when she and Charlie were little more than babies? You think Kitty is going to break her mother's heart and move to the other side of the world?' He paused, one wild eyebrow raised. When Sammy hesitated, Uncle Geoff continued. 'No, I thought so – this is all about you and what you want. Kitty's young, she has her whole life ahead of her. You hardly even know her.'

Sammy had fallen quiet in the face of Uncle Geoff's tirade, but at this he steadied himself and looked him in the eye.

'I know Kitty. I know her better than I've known anyone in my entire life. I know I love her and I know that she loves me.'

Uncle Geoff banged his fist on the gatepost.

'Leave her alone!'

Sammy stepped away from the gate, his face stricken with anguish.

'Will you tell her I came to see her?'

'Get along with you now – I've got things to do.'

Sammy walked away and Uncle Geoff watched him go.

Bert saw Sammy sitting on the wing of his plane, his back curled and his head bent over. As Bert walked towards him he saw that he was writing.

'That you, Bailey? They sent you here or what?' Bert squinted into the sun.

Sammy looked down and Bert was shocked. He was used to seeing men's faces altered by fear and fatigue, but this was something else.

August 2006

Kitty sleeps with Sammy's letter beneath her pillow. She dreams that she is with him and they are young. He kisses her goodbye and she wakes. In her mind she sees him clearly: he is waiting for her just as he promises in his letter. As dawn comes, Kitty stands at the open window with the folded pages in her hands. She listens to the birdsong and imagines she hears other sounds: the rumble of a truck convoy, reveille played on a distant bugle. And then she hears the ghost of a clatter downstairs and Aunt Vi is in the kitchen baking bread while Uncle Geoff sits at the table, slowly turning the pages of his newspaper. It is not her vinyl-floored marble-surfaced modern room that Kitty sees, but the stone floor and distempered brick walls of the kitchen as it was sixty years ago. And she hears the screech of Charlie's brakes as his bicycle arrives at the gate. *My poor brother,* Kitty thinks, and she wonders if Charlie ever knew about Sammy.

The question stirs her and Kitty turns from the window with a plan forming in her mind. She dresses and while eating her breakfast she considers what she should do for the best. As the morning wears on, she potters about the house thinking of Charlie. At last she decides. Moving from the kitchen with sudden purposefulness, Kitty picks up her bag and takes her keys from the hall stand. She will visit Charlie and ask him what he remembers, find out what he knows.

Kitty reverses her car out into the lane. She drives for forty minutes before turning the car into the long drive. Gravel shifts beneath the tyres. Shadow, then yellow sunlight, then shadow fall on her as the car flits past the beech trees that line the road. Ahead of her, the house sits above a sloping lawn. Kitty pulls into a bay marked 'visitors' parking' and climbs out of the car beside a bush that is heavy with bees.

* * *

When they found Charlie in 1944, he was in a bad way. He had lost weight, having had little to eat in three weeks, and he had been involved in a fight. Aunt Vi soon fattened him up and his bruises faded but the greatest change in Charlie was not physical. He was silent and secretive; he had no enthusiasm for anything and if Kitty tried to talk to him he simply gazed at her before looking away. She wonders if she could have tried harder to reach Charlie. But she recalls how sullen he had been and the worry he had caused their mother, and how she had swung between feeling afraid for him and angry with him.

In the spacious lobby, Kitty is drawn to a water cooler. Her shoes make a pleasing sound as she crosses the tiled floor. She pulls a waxed-paper cone from a dispenser and fills it with iced water. The machine glugs as it refills.

'Hello, Mrs Poll.'

Kitty turns and greets a tall woman. She is not in uniform but a plastic identification card bearing her photograph swings on its beaded chain around her neck.

'Mr Danby is in the dining room – it's lunchtime.'

Kitty checks her watch.

'Oh, yes of course it is. I wasn't thinking. I can wait for him.'

'Why don't you go on up? I'll pop into the dining room and let him know that you're here.'

Kitty climbs the curving staircase and walks along the corridor to Charlie's room. He has left the door open and she pauses for a moment before going in. Sunshine pours through the open window and lights half the carpet, a slice of Charlie's neatly-made bed and a dusty triangle of his wardrobe. Kitty goes over to the mantelpiece and picks up the carved wooden bear and cradles it in her hands. She remembers how, after the war, Charlie could not settle to anything. He took temporary jobs and he moved from town to town. For over ten years he drifted. He was arrested again and again for vagrancy, for being drunk and disorderly. Kitty feels sadness constrict her throat as she remembers driving to collect him from a police station with her mother weeping beside her.

'He can't go on like this Kitty – he can't.'

She is still holding the wooden bear when Charlie comes into the room.

'Hello, Charlie,' Kitty says as she turns to him and replaces the bear.

Charlie crosses to where she stands and moves the bear slightly to the left of where Kitty has put it and rotates it slowly through thirty degrees. Kitty touches his arm and repeats the greeting.

'Hello, Kit,' Charlie says at last. Kitty looks at his broad face, his dark, widely-spaced eyes like her own. She notices, as always, but with a renewed stab of sadness, the squashed asymmetry of his much broken nose, the pink groove of a scar that runs from his scalp to the corner of his left eye, the puckered bulbous skin of his damaged ears. It is a face that would frighten children.

Beneath the open window there is a small table and two chairs. Kitty goes and sits on the wooden chair and gestures towards the armchair.

'Come and sit down, Charlie.'

And, as he lumbers over and sinks into the chair, Kitty remembers the old Charlie; the little, round-faced brother who followed her and was quick to laugh and quick to cry. Then she recalls Charlie as he was in the early months of 1944. He was a strong, capable teenager, who had suddenly grown much bigger than her. And, looking back, Kitty recalls his burgeoning patriotism and his sense of justice and thinks she sees a youth on the cusp of being a very fine man. But they lost Charlie after the bomb fell at Broughton's farm. That Charlie witnessed a horror from which he never recovered.

'Charlie,' Kitty begins cautiously, 'I've been thinking about the war. About Sammy. Do you remember Sammy, Charlie?'

Charlie moves his back against the chair and looks to the window where a large fly buzzes and bangs against the glass. Kitty waits for a moment and tries again.

'I've been talking to Bert Wright. He was at the airbase. Do you remember Bert, Charlie? He's ninety-three now.'

'Sammy was a Mustang pilot.' Charlie looks at her and smiles.

'Yes, yes he was.'

'You kissed him.' Charlie grins and for a moment Kitty feels that they are young again.

'Were you spying on us, Charlie Danby?' she asks, daring to tease him.

Charlie becomes serious. He frowns and looks down at his hands. 'Mrs Parkes saw you,' he says

194

quietly. Then louder, 'She told Uncle Geoff.'

Kitty gazes at Charlie and begins to nod.

'It's all right, Charlie, I remember that Uncle Geoff didn't like Sammy. That just helps me understand why Sammy went away ' Kitty breaks off. She wants to tell Charlie that it was Sammy who shot down the V1.

'Charlie, Bert told me something that I didn't know . . . about Sammy.' She pauses as she tries to anticipate Charlie's reaction to what she is about to tell him. She does not want to upset him, but nor does she want to collude in a deceit. Kitty leans forward and places her hand on top of Charlie's. The fly bounces repeatedly off the window; if it flew down a few inches, it would be free. Kitty carries on because she must.

'Charlie, when the V1 exploded it was shot down by a fighter pilot, by an American fighter pilot.'

Slowly, Charlie turns his eyes to her face and he is attentive. There is, she thinks, no going back now.

'It was a Mustang and —'

But Charlie interrupts. He speaks loudly. '— with Browning fifty-calibre machine guns in the wings, four of them in all, angled towards each other so that the bullets converged on a target thirty yards ahead of the prop. The two outer guns carried two hundred and eighty rounds, the inner two were loaded with three hundred and fifty rounds each. Every tenth bullet was a tracer bullet; they showed up white so that the pilot could see if his aim was true.' Charlie stops and waits for Kitty to speak.

'Yes, I didn't know that. But the thing that Bert told me was that it was Sammy who shot down the V1. Sammy was the pilot, Charlie. It was Sammy who brought the V1 down.'

Kitty feels the pressure build behind her eyes, but she will not cry. She watches her brother and she seeks reassurance. She needs to know that this news has not hurt him. Charlie reaches out and places his hands beneath the sash window and raises it slightly. A moment later the fly dips down from the pane and is gone, speeding into the sunlight. Then he lifts Kitty's hand from the table and holds it in his.

'It wasn't Sammy. You mustn't think it was Sammy. It was Hitler. Hitler did it, Kit, not your Sammy.'

And Kitty cannot hold back any longer and she begins to cry. Charlie gets up from his chair and goes to her. He stands beside her for a moment, big and awkward, and then he leans over her and places his arm heavily across her shoulders. Kitty has not expected that it will turn out like this, with Charlie comforting her. And she thinks that it is the relief that has made her cry. And hearing Charlie say the words 'your Sammy'. And, more than anything, the feeling that, after sixty long years of his being lost to her, she has found her brother again.

June 1944

Win Danby arrived before she was expected, having talked her way on to a goods train at Victoria Station and getting a lift in the back of an army vehicle from Ashford to Charing Heath. She walked the rest of the way and tapped at the back door shortly before six in the morning. Her brother was making up the fire under the copper in the kitchen and he straightened up and opened the door.

'Blimey, Win, you're early,' he said as she kissed his cheek and came into the room. He went to take her bag from her, but she was too quick for him and had carried it through to the hallway and returned to the kitchen by the time he had closed the door. She looked tired and anxious.

'How's Kitty? Any news of Charlie?' She leaned into the fire and warmed her hands.

Geoff sighed. 'Kitty's very poorly but they don't think it is diphtheria. The doctor's coming again this morning. As for Charlie, there's been no word. Someone thought they saw him in Ashford but it was a false alarm.'

Vi came into the kitchen carrying a tray which she put down on the table. She hugged her sister-in-law.

'Kitty's awake. She's had a better night.'

Win kneeled at her daughter's bedside and smiled as the tears welled in Kitty's eyes and flooded to the pillow.

'Hello, my darling – don't cry, love. I'm here.'

'Oh Mum,' Kitty croaked, 'everything's gone wrong.'

'Hush, love – it's going to be all right. You'll get better and we'll find Charlie, you'll see. It'll soon be right again.'

But later, after the doctor had been, Kitty heard Uncle Geoff and her mum arguing. When Aunt Vi came into the room, Kitty overheard her mum call Uncle Geoff a ruddy fool through the open door.

'What's wrong?' she managed to whisper, wincing with pain.

'Oh, never you mind, love, you're not to worry. Uncle Geoff doesn't like change and he's a bit upset, that's all. And, between you and me, I don't think he knows what to make of your mum wearing trousers and coming out with the odd swear word. He's her big brother and he likes to tell her what to do. And, though he's too old to fight and he knows that farm labouring and market gardening is important war work, I think he feels a bit put out that it's your mum who's in the uniform and doing a man's job.' She sat beside Kitty and shook a bottle of medicine.

'Don't forget, your Uncle Geoff was your dad's best friend, they went through a lot together in the last war – dear me, terrible it was for them, terrible. After your dad died, Geoff's always been trying to look after your mum. But he goes about it in the wrong way – always criticising her, he can't help himself. He tried to get her to move down here with us when you were little, but she wouldn't have it.'

Aunt Vi slipped her arm behind Kitty's shoulders

and raised a spoonful of the thick brown medicine to her lips. 'Yes, she certainly knows her own mind, does your mum.' She leaned forward and kissed Kitty's forehead before screwing the lid back on the bottle.

'Now, I'll just change the sheets on the camp bed. Mum's going to stay with you from now on.'

After their bad start, Win and Geoff kept out of each other's way. Uncle Geoff took to rising earlier than usual and contrived to be hardly ever at home; finding one excuse or another to be out of the house. Each morning he went to the farm for milk and then to the police station to see if there was any news of Charlie. On the way back he popped into the post office and collected the post.

Kitty gradually got better, and one day she was well enough for her mother to help her out to the garden where she sat in the sun wearing an old, wide-brimmed straw hat of Aunt Vi's.

'Raspberries and cream. Get you fattened up a bit.' Win smiled at her daughter as she put a bowl into her hands. 'Then there's some peas to shell for tea tonight – we can do them together.'

They both looked up and squinted into the sun as Uncle Geoff arrived suddenly at the gate.

'We've found Charlie – he's in Portsmouth!'

'Portsmouth? Is he all right?'

Uncle Geoff rolled his head and hunched his shoulders as Win approached him, and Kitty strained to hear what he said next but caught only the word 'fight'. Kitty placed the bowl on the ground beside her chair and got to her feet. Nearly three weeks in bed had left her weak and she held her hands out to the side in order to steady herself. She shuffled forward clumsily, her feet unable to anticipate when they would touch the ground.

'What's happened to Charlie? Please tell me.' She swayed then and tottered towards them and her mother and uncle rushed forward to catch her.

'He's fine – I'm going to Portsmouth to pick him up,' Uncle Geoff said.

'*We're* going to Portsmouth – you'll be all right with Auntie Vi, won't you, Kitty?'

Kitty nodded and they helped her to her chair.

After they left, Aunt Vi brought another chair and settled herself beside Kitty. They sat quietly for several minutes, then Kitty asked her aunt if she had heard anything from Sammy while she had been ill.

'I don't know why he's stopped writing to me and I'm afraid.'

Aunt Vi took her hand and squeezed it.

'I'm sorry, dear. I think that perhaps you had better try not to think about him any more. Best put it behind you.'

Kitty gulped a lungful of air and tears sprang from her eyes. 'I can't, Auntie Vi, I can't stop thinking about him. I miss him so much it hurts, and I don't think I can bear it if anything has happened to him.'

'Shh, now come on. I know it hurts now but you'll get over it, you'll see.'

'I don't want to get over it! I love him.'

Kitty abandoned herself to her crying then and Aunt Vi took her in her arms and held her.

'Look now, come on, lovey, I tell you what we'll do – but you're to stop crying now, you hear me?'

It took some time before Kitty's sobs subsided but at last she was quiet, and Vi put her hand under her chin and tipped her face up so that she could see her properly.

'I want you to get back into bed now and rest, and I'll go to the airbase and ask after Sammy and see what I can find out. All right, Kitty? You be a good girl for me and I'll be back as soon as I can.'

Kitty sniffed and murmured her thanks as Aunt Vi helped her to her feet.

Kitty lay curled beneath the sheets and blankets and thought about Sammy and waited for Aunt Vi to return. As her mind wandered, she swung from hope to despair and back again. She imagined Aunt Vi bringing good news, then bad, then good. She didn't expect to fall asleep but her thoughts soon exhausted her. She woke with a start an hour later to find Aunt Vi standing by her bed.

'Tell me,' Kitty pleaded as she struggled to sit up.

Aunt Vi sat down on the bed. She held a book in her hands which she placed in Kitty's lap.

'I'm sorry, love – I've no news, there's only this.'

September 2006

Kitty wakes and immediately senses that the season has changed and autumn has come. She rises and bathes then goes to the kitchen. She is making tea when the post falls to the mat. She walks through the hall to the front door and sees a blue airmail envelope and sighs. So, it isn't over yet – she hasn't heard the last of John F. Bailey Rowe. But then she smiles, because part of her is pleased that this young person wants to know more of her past.

As she picks up the letter, she sees that the handwriting is different. Different yet familiar and as she turns it over, she reads the sender's name –

Mr S. R. Bailey – and she exclaims aloud. She places her hand against the wall to steady herself. *But Sammy is dead*, she thinks. And then she wonders how she knows this. *Who said that he was dead?* And she cannot remember.

Kitty hurries to her chair by the window and the starlings take off from the lawn. She opens the letter with trembling fingers. As she pulls the airmail pages from the envelope she sees, tucked behind them, a greetings card. On its cover is a picture of bluebirds that spell out the words *Thank you* by the way they have settled on a telegraph wire. Kitty puts the letter in her lap and opens the card. It is from John F. Bailey Rowe.

Dear Mrs Poll,

I am writing to thank you for sending me all the cool facts about Mustangs and telling me about the things Grandpa did in the war. He is really pleased that I wrote you and I'm glad about that too, because I could have gotten into trouble with my mom. When I started my project, Mom said I couldn't worry Grandpa with it because he had a terrible time in the war and he never talks about it. But I did have his pilot's logbook and I could just make out your name and address pencilled in the back of it. I didn't really expect to get a reply to be honest, but I knew I'd get a research merit for trying (I kind of need all the merits I can get right now). Anyhow, you did reply – yay for you! And I'm in the unusual situation of being praised at school and at home and I've got you to thank for that.

Best wishes
John Francis

Kitty looks again at the picture on the front of the card and shakes her head and smiles before turning her attention to the letter. She opens it carefully. And as she pulls the paper free she is overwhelmed with tenderness. For everything about it is familiar to her: the feel of the paper, the way it is folded and the handwriting. It is looser and a little shakier, but it is undoubtedly Sammy's handwriting.

My dearest darling Kitty,

There seems to be no other way to start a letter to you, though some would say that I hardly know you – but you are my darling dearest Kitty and will ever remain so. I imagine that you had a shock when Johnny wrote you and I daresay this letter from me will now be another. What I want to tell you straight away is that I was warned to stay away from you by your Uncle Geoff and I think he would have done anything to stop me marrying you and I am sorry that I let him get the better of me. I hope that you can forgive me Kitty. I found out, in 1956, that your Uncle Geoff had intercepted my letter to you – so I also know that you must have been very let down and wondering why I disappeared without a word. Maybe you thought that I was dead or, worse, had met someone else, but I can honestly tell you there never was and never has been anyone else for me. In your letter to Johnny you mention the poetry book and a photograph. I couldn't think what it was for a while and then I remembered. I hate thinking about you having that picture and thinking it was important to me. But the fact is that in 1956 I did get married – not to the girl in the picture but to her sister. Flick was real keen and everyone expected it and I think I must have been sleepwalking while Flick chattered on and arranged our wedding. All I could think about was you Kitty and in the end I told

Flick that I'd got cold feet. In my last letter to you I said that I'd wait for you to say the word, but I decided then that I had to find you and ask you again face to face and then I'd know.

So that's when I came to England. I figured that you would have moved back to London but in any case I only had your Aunt and Uncle's place in Kent to go on so I went there. I thought that all I needed to do was win round your Uncle Geoff then maybe there would be a chance for us. I hoped that the passing of time would have made it easier between him and me. Well, as you know, by that time Uncle Geoff had been dead some years and I realised from what your Aunt Vi said that you hadn't received the letter I left with Bert. It was a terrible blow to me Kitty. Your Aunt Vi was pretty distressed too – I don't think she knew what Geoff had done. I wanted to see you but Vi convinced me not to. She told me that you were married and that you were happy so I gave you up. I came straight back home and went ahead and married Flick.

Well, I'm sad to say it didn't work out for me and Flick and we got divorced in 1972 or thereabouts. We've got a great couple of kids though, Dawn and

Sally and I've got five grandchildren and Dawn's eldest Jessica is expecting a baby in November so before the year is out I'll be a great grand-daddy. In your letter to Johnny you mention being widowed and I'm really sorry to hear that. I hope that you and your husband had many good years before he died and I pray that he was good to you. I wonder about your life – if you had children. God there's so much I want to know about you Kitty and I hope that you will write to me and tell me about yourself. I'm terrified that I'm going to be too late – that something might happen to you between me posting this and it getting to you. I'm pleased to say that I'm still fit and healthy but since Johnny came over with your letter I've been feeling sick one minute and giddy the next. So, what I was going to ask you is, if you feel you can do it, maybe you could phone me. The number's at the top of this letter and I'm going to stay home day and night like a love-sick college boy just in case.

Ever yours,
Sammy

PS: I'm still living in the old place and the cabin is still there down by the river – you remember the cabin Kitty?

Kitty finishes the letter and reads it again from the beginning. Then she goes to the telephone and calls her daughter.

'Hello dear, it's Mum.'

She listens quietly.

'That's good dear – you're always so busy. Now darling, can you tell me? Is this a good time to phone America? . . . Pardon? . . . Oh, Pennsylvania.'

She pauses and listens.

'I've just received a wonderful letter from an old friend – someone very, very dear to me . . . Is it a good time or not? . . . Oh. Well, what time should I ring then?'

Kitty hangs up the phone and sits staring at the letter. It would be a ridiculous thing to do to wake him up in the middle of the night. And she reasons that after sixty-two years she can wait another few hours. She stares at the phone for a little while and then lifts the receiver and dials.

Kitty listens to the unfamiliar ring tone and waits.

At last it is answered and she hears a clunk and some fumbling and then a voice says, 'Hello?'

Kitty catches her breath. She places her hand on her throat; she is crying and unsure how her voice will come out.

'Hello?' he says again.

'Hello, Sammy – it's Kitty. I got your letter.'

Afterword

This story is fiction but it was inspired by a real event that occurred during the Second World War. On 25th June 1944, fifty-two members of the 6th Guards Tank Brigade Workshop Royal Electrical and Mechanical Engineers, who were stationed between Lenham and Charing in Kent, were killed by a flying bomb. My father survived.

KATE
LE VANN

Things
I Know
About
Love

Livia's experience of love has been disappointing to say the least. But all that is about to change. After years of illness, she's off to spend the summer with her brother in America. She's making up for lost time, and she's writing it all down in her private blog. America is everything she's dreamed of – and then she meets Adam. Can Livia put the past behind her and risk falling in love again?

'Compelling and compassionate . . . a moving and gentle awareness of a real relationship.' *Carousel*

DAMIAN KELLEHER

LIFE, INTERRUPTED

Luke's world is turned upside down when his mum collapses at the hospital where she works as a nurse. Fourteen-year-old Luke and his football-obssessed younger brother Jesse each cope in their different ways, and, as time passes, they confront some painful truths. Honest, funny and deeply moving, this is a story about facing the worst and surviving.

'Warm and funny - though searingly sad at times. I wish I'd written it.'
Jacqueline Wilson

☆

www.piccadillypress.co.uk

☆ The latest news on forthcoming books

☆ Chapter previews

☆ Author biographies

☆ Fun quizzes

☆ Reader reviews

☆ Competitions and fab prizes

☆ Book features and cool downloads

☆ And much, much more . . .

Log on and check it out!

Piccadilly Press

☆